"It's disconcerting to have someone know your thoughts," she said.

"It makes me feel so vulnerable and naked . . ."

"I would love to see you vulnerable and naked." He moved his lips down her neck, pushing her long auburn hair aside. "I've thought of nothing else all day."

She trembled, realizing that she felt the same way.

"My God, you are beautiful, Ariane. I want to possess your very soul."

It was insane, foolish. And yet she wanted Jacques at that moment more than she had ever wanted anyone or anything in her life.

Second Chance at Love

HARD TO HANDLE
SUSANNA COLLINS

A JOVE BOOK

First Jove edition published October 1981

First printing

"Second Chance at Love" and the butterfly emblem are trademarks be-
longing to Jove Publications, Inc.

Printed in the United States of America

Jove books are published by Jove Publications, Inc.,
200 Madison Avenue, New York, NY 10016

HARD TO HANDLE

Chapter One

ARIANE TRIED TO keep her voice low and steady as the thoroughbred danced wildly in place.

"Easy now, Willie."

The Antwerp harbor official seemed surprised to see such a tiny young woman handling the large, unruly stallion. "Need some help with him?"

"No, thanks, I can manage."

The man shrugged with an air of disbelief and motioned for her to start down the ship's ramp.

She pushed a strand of long, thick auburn hair from her eyes and patted Wicked Willie's neck. "Here we go, Will. Don't let me down. Oh, please, don't let me down." She drew in her breath and pulled gently on the lead rope.

The horse quickly sensed her fear. His muscles were as tense as Ariane's. He took a few tentative steps, then stopped. "If only Bud were here," she said under her breath. How many times had she uttered that phrase in the last few months, she wondered. The absurdity was that if Bud were still alive, she would not be in Belgium trying to coax their prize stallion down a ship's ramp.

She started forward again, glancing down at the hooves pounding the floor of the ramp. She felt dizzy, as if she were looking down from the heights of a skyscraper. She trembled visibly, and the stallion, again sensing her fear, reared up, his hooves landing inches from her feet.

She chastised herself, aware that a few months ago she would have been a rock in this situation. There wasn't a horse in the world who could frighten her, and now she felt like one big feverish mass of nerves with a horse she'd raised from a colt.

A man was coming quickly toward them up the ramp. In his early thirties, he was wearing riding pants and long black boots, a forest-green turtleneck sweater and a brown tweed jacket. Though she was concentrating on Willie, Ariane could not help but notice his strikingly handsome features, jet-black hair, and high, chiseled cheekbones set wide apart. He had the pale complexion of the Pays-Bas, the Low Countries, though a healthy, ruddy tinge to his cheeks told her he spent a good deal of time out of doors. As he approached, she was riveted by his large green eyes fringed with black lashes under straight dark eyebrows. The contrast against his pale skin gave him a dramatic, almost reckless look, though the rest of his well-muscled body moved with calm, civilized assurance.

"Mrs. Charles?" he asked her.

"Yes?"

"I'm Jacques Valbonne. And this charming creature must be the famous Wicked Willie. *Bonjour, Guillaume le Méchant.*"

In spite of her turmoil, Ariane couldn't help smiling at the loose French translation of Willie's name, reminding her as it did of French schoolchildren calling out "*Méchant!*" to others who had done them wrong. She chuckled. "The *in*famous Wicked Willie, I'd call him at this point."

"He is living up to his name," Jacques said, laughing, and patted Willie's long neck.

Thankfully the horse seemed to become calmer in the man's presence. Ariane knew *she* was.

"He's really not like this." She felt obliged to apologize for the stallion's erratic behavior.

He nodded in understanding. "They're all like this coming off a ship. Everything is new and frightening."

"I guess I should have given him a tranquilizer," she added, "but I've always avoided using drugs with him."

"I'm glad you didn't." He patted Willie's neck again. "I only use them as a last resort, and I don't think he'll be any trouble. I've seen a lot worse."

Ariane gratefully relinquished the lead rope to Jacques, and he took over with the expert movements of a man who knows horses well. When Willie refused to budge, he slapped the horse on the chest. It was not a hard slap, but one loud enough to make the horse pay attention, to spur him forward. *"Eh bien, mon vieux, allons!"* His tone of voice as well as the words themselves urged the horse forward.

Willie took a few steps down the ramp, ready to put his trust in this reassuring stranger, but a sudden commotion of horses at the base of the ramp frightened him, and he reared again dangerously. Jacques calmly leaned back to avoid having the powerful hooves crash into his head.

The remembered terror gripped Ariane's chest. She shut her eyes, unable to watch. A scream hovered at the back of her throat, but she held it in for fear the noise would further inflame the horse.

When she opened her eyes, Jacques was easily leading a docile, obedient Wicked Willie down the ramp. Ariane breathed freely again and unclenched her fists. "Thank heaven, it's finally over," she muttered. "Good-bye, Will; good-bye, horses."

She wished there were some way she could simply walk away at that moment, but there were transfer papers and bills of lading to sign. And she felt some obligation to help Willie get settled in the trailer that was finally to take him out of her life.

She was pleased to see that it was a luxurious, custom-designed horse trailer with thick padding on the sides, kept immaculately clean. The hay in the feeder was of the finest quality. As Ariane unhooked his halter, she scratched Willie's ears and whispered, "Willie, you're going to be living better than I am!"

Patting him one last time, she found herself biting her lower lip to keep away the tears. For months she had thought of nothing but ridding herself of the horses, but now that the last one, her favorite, was leaving she felt inexplicably sad. All her fond memories of the scruffy, playful little colt, the same color as her own auburn hair, flooded back. She thought of the day he was born, and of all the shows and blue ribbons she had won with him.

"He's a good horse," she said as she turned to Jacques Valbonne awkwardly. "Your sister will enjoy him. I hope he brings her as much pleasure as he did me."

"She has spoken of nothng but this Wicked Willie since she returned from America."

"He'll work very hard for you. He's a real performer at heart, loves the applause. Well, good luck. It was nice meeting you, Monsieur Valbonne. My regards to your sister."

She turned to walk away, but he took her arm. "Where are you going?"

Her large brown eyes met his as his question forced her to face him. "I thought I'd take the train to Brussels, then to Paris. I have an aunt there."

"But Danielle is expecting you to spend a few days with us. She will be very disappointed if you don't come to Bruges," he said quickly. "You are expected in Paris?"

"Not immediately. My aunt knows I am arriving in Europe and expects me to visit. I have no set plans, but . . .".

Before she could protest, he had taken her suitcase and placed it in the truck. "It would be a pity to come to Europe and not see Bruges. It's the most beautiful city in Europe." He was holding the door open for her, and she looked up again into his dark green eyes. There was something mysteriously compelling about them, so captivating that she found herself accepting his invitation as unquestioningly as Willie had followed him on the ramp.

He took his place in the driver's seat and put the truck in gear.

"Danielle told me about you when she was in New York," Ariane said in a friendly attempt at conversation as they pulled out of the harbor area.

"What did my sister say about me?" He raised his dark eyebrows, while a smile played in the depths of his green eyes. It was a sensuous look that unnerved her for a moment. Danielle had certainly not prepared her for the virile sexuality this man possessed.

"You are an excellent trainer, she told me."

"Excellent? I don't know"—he smiled at the compliment—"but I am very good. Horses are my life. My father claims I love them more than my life." He had a low, deeply accented voice, but it did not remind her of the flowery French of perfume commercials. There was a masculine ruggedness in the rich tones that suggested the throaty voices of the stallions he trained. "You are in the horse business, too, are you not?"

"I *was* a trainer. So was my late husband."

"Yes, Danielle told me you were a recent widow. I am very sorry. But I pictured you as a white-haired old lady dressed in black. I had no idea you were so young and pretty."

"Twenty-seven is not really that young, and though I hate to admit it, I am beginning to find strands of gray in my hair."

"You look much younger," he commented.

She knew that it was not just an idle compliment, for she did look younger than her years. It had been an unwelcome blessing when she was growing up and desperately wanted Bud to notice her, but now she was grateful for her youthful looks.

She had flawlessly smooth, fair skin, and vigorous daily physical work around the horses had given her a lithe, well-toned body. Her hair was an unusual red shade of auburn, and when not riding in shows she let it flow loosely, cascading in soft waves onto her shoulders. Knowing that her thick hair was her best feature, she tried to choose clothes to accent it, and the rust colors of autumn suited her well, setting off the rich color of her hair and her large, dark brown eyes. Before leaving New York she had gone on an impulsive buying spree, indulging in wild, fashionable clothes she would never have considered while she was married to Bud. In those days all the money budgeted for clothes had gone into riding outfits for shows. That morning she'd taken advantage of her new wardrobe, having donned a deep rust colored silk blouse with feminine, billowy sleeves and shapely pants to match. It was obvious Jacques Valbonne had noted the woman *and* the clothes with pleasure. He was a man who appreciated beauty in all things, Ariane sensed—especially in women and horses.

"Your husband, how did he die?"

The abrupt, personal question startled her. She would have preferred not to discuss Bud's death, but as she politely though briefly described the riding accident to Jacques, she found that for the first time in months she could speak of it without choking up. Was time healing the wounds, or was there something about Jacques that put her, like Wicked Willie, at ease?

"They are dangerous animals, horses," Jacques commented thoughtfully when she finished the story. "My mother also died from a fall. I think those of us who love horses are more than a little crazy."

"Count *me* out. I'm through with them forever."

"Because of the accident?" He gazed at her with surprise. "You look to me like a woman of courage."

She did not want to admit to him the terror she now felt around horses. But there was more that she didn't mind one bit admitting to.

"Bud's death made me sit back and reevaluate my life. Ever since I can remember, horses were all I cared about. When I was a little girl, all my dolls had their own horses. I was thirteen when I began riding lessons. Bud was my instructor, and by nineteen, I'd married him."

"It must have been a beautiful marriage." He spoke the words with deep conviction.

"Why do you say that?"

"To build a life around horses—they are the most emotional of any animal and give so much of themselves, so much love. When a man and woman share in that and love each other, it must be a perfect marriage."

Ariane winced. "There is a lot of hard work involved," she said with more bitterness than she actually felt. "Stalls to muck out in the winter, keeping the horses vetted and clipped and exercised when you're dog-tired. We had a riding academy as well as a breeding farm and boarding stable. I used to teach three classes a day—yelling commands at sassy, uncoordinated kids. Then there was getting up at four o'clock in the morning to bathe and groom the horses for a show. I'm sure not going to miss any of that!"

"No?" He pinned her briefly with his green eyes, fringed with black lashes, and she knew in that instant that he saw through her pretense. She had done all that hard work joyfully and would have continued to do it. But since the accident she was no longer able to work with the horses she loved. The minute she was seated in a saddle the horrible vision of Bud's accident came back to her. Knees shaking, sick to her stomach, trembling with fear, she could not ride. In the end, there had been no other choice but to sell the farm and look for a new life.

And yet she was not in any mood to reveal this to the handsome stranger who seemed to see through her. "I forget, monsieur, you are one of them," she teased him brightly, "—the 'horse people' who don't find anything unbearable as long as it has to do with those precious animals!"

He grinned. "I confess. Your husband was like that also?"

"He was the original. Sometimes I think he only married me to have an extra trainer and teacher on staff."

She'd meant to sound as if she were joking, but apparently she hadn't succeeded. Jacques picked up the serious undertone in what she'd said.

"You don't really believe that a man would marry a girl as beautiful as you simply to have another trainer?"

His comment surprised her. Was there anything she could hide from this man? There *had* been a nagging doubt throughout most of her marriage, though she had never dared discuss it with anyone. Bud had never shown any great affection for her, though he lavished attention on his prize horses. But then neither had he given her any reason to doubt his love. He had been too occupied day and night with the horses to maintain any romantic liaison. After the

first few years of marriage, she simply excused his coolness to her, labeling him an undemonstrative man.

"It was a terrific marriage," she managed to say in a
tone she hoped carried conviction. "I mean, how could it
fail with so much in common between us?"

"Could it?" Jacques was not easily taken in.

"Well, it *didn't*," she said with irritation. What business
was it of his to be probing into her personal life?

"Then what were your doubts?" he asked calmly, ignoring her discomfort.

"There were no doubts, it's just that..."

"What?"

"Nothing."

"You wondered perhaps if he loved the horses more
than he loved you?"

"What a ridiculous thing to ask." She looked sharply
away from his penetrating gaze. She could not let him
know that he was right. It would be a humiliating confession for a widow to admit that her husband might not have
loved her—that he might have used her because of her
equestrian skills.

"Then what was not right about the marriage?"

"Who said there was something wrong?"

"You're angry with me for asking these questions?"

"Not at all," she snapped. "Every marriage has its ups
and downs. The only thing that might have been better
was if we'd had children." Actually she and Bud had never
tried to have them. There had been too much work at the
farm to consider taking on the extra responsibility of a
family, but she realized that she had to provide Jacques
Valbonne with a satisfactory answer to his probing questions. He obviously was not a person who would let go
of a subject once it was broached. And she knew from his
reputation that he was the kind of trainer who never gave
up on a difficult horse. Oh yes, he was the type who would
always get what he was after.

Jacques nodded, satisfied for the moment with her response. "I cannot imagine any marriage really complete
without children. They're wonderful little creatures." He

smiled in a mysterious, wistful way that made Ariane think that he was probably referring tô one in particular. Perhaps his own?

"Have you ever been married, Jacques?"

"No. I was close once, about ten years ago. But it was just the opposite from you. I loved the girl, but she despised horses and I was afraid the passion would never sustain itself if we had nothing in common."

Ariane gazed at the handsome man sitting next to her, his black hair blowing in the wind from the open window. There was something of the untamed savage in the face of this Belgian aristocrat: a wild streak one found in thoroughbreds with even the best of bloodlines. She had seen that spark one day in a newborn foal, and she named him Wicked Willie because of it. The trick to training those brazen animals, she knew, was to teach them manners without breaking their spirits. Someone had managed it with Jacques Valbonne.

As they drove she could not help making comparisons between Jacques and Bud. The prime moving force in both men's lives, horses, was exactly the same. And though Jacques's face was infinitely more handsome, she knew the bodies would be the same—the strong shoulders and backs, the long muscled legs, and, especially, the hard thighs that were so essential to gripping a horse. It was a body that, like the thoroughbred's, had been disciplined by the demanding rigors of the sport. What separated Bud from Jacques, she decided as she watched him, was the streak of fire that coursed through the Belgian's veins, the promise of volcanic passion seething just beneath the surface.

Bud had never presented her with any startling revelations about his character. What was on the surface penetrated to the depths. He had been calm, reliable, reassuring. And she had accepted him without question, considered herself lucky to have him, just as others did. How often friends had said she was the luckiest of women to have such a "perfect marriage."

Jacques broke into her thoughts. "And now that you

are finished with horses, what are you going to do with your life?"

"There is a whole world out there I want to know and experience. I want to travel. I want to read books on astronomy and economics and history. I want to go to concerts and discos and operas and buy silly clothes in Paris boutiques. All the things I've wondered about, never had time for. And I want..." she paused, her eyes dancing. Should she tell him?

"A lover?"

She knew the word was tossed around in French with much greater abandon than in English, but she did not want him to think that she planned to flit from one bed to the next like some debauched thrill-seeker.

"There has been only one man in my life," she said a bit stiffly. "Maybe that's odd in this day and age, but I never wanted anyone other than Bud. We always got along well, but it was never what you'd call a... well, *romantic* relationship, what with worrying about the horses and shows. I guess I've always had a silly schoolgirl notion... Why are you looking at me that way?"

He was grinning. "Let me tell you what you are wishing for: bouquets of lilacs tied with a ribbon, candlelit dinners for two, the romantic clink of champagne glasses, a tropical sunset."

"You make it sound like a travel brochure!"

"Isn't that what you have in mind?"

"Yes." She smiled sheepishly. "Maybe there is no such thing, but I'd just like to see for myself."

"It's there, Ariane. And you are beautiful enough to find a man to give that to you." He gave her an indolent look from under his dark lashes, and she felt uneasy. There was no room for doubt about what he was feeling. The communication between them at that moment was overpowering.

A brief silence followed, which he broke with another playful grin. "But it will not be me who will fulfill your romantic notions, *ma chère*." He reached over and touched her cheek.

"Why not?" She was amazed at her own boldness and taken off guard by the startling effect of his touch.

"You may be my style, but candlelight definitely is not."

"What is your style," she teased, "broad daylight?"

He laughed. "Yes. I do not like a girl who has anything to hide. I prefer to make love with all the lights on, don't you?"

She glanced nervously out the window. The conversation was rapidly careening out of control. Jacques Valbonne was certainly not like any man she'd ever met. It would be wiser not to encourage him. It was apparent that he was the kind of man who might drive the truck over to the side of the road and lead her out to some meadow to make love. She cleared her throat. "This is beautiful countryside."

"People never think of Belgium as picturesque," he responded, picking up the new topic of conversation as though nothing had happened. "People come to Europe on twenty-one-day tours of twenty-two countries. What was that funny movie that came out a few years ago?"

"If It's Tuesday, It Must Be Belgium," she supplied.

"That's it. They spend one night in Brussels and then leave the next morning. They never come to Flanders."

"Flanders?"

"Northern Belgium. It's quite different from the south. The Flemish landscapes are unique in all the world. One can always recognize them in art museums because there is more sky than land in the pictures. Our country is so flat that it brings the sky down to us and we live intimately with the clouds."

The vague mass of countryside suddenly took detailed shape for Ariane, and she wondered how she had managed to miss the obvious. The great gray and white clouds had a massive, dramatic presence, swirling in heavy cotton patterns, dipping so low over the tiled rooftops she felt she could almost reach up and touch them.

Something of the awestruck child she had once been reawakened in her. How many years had it been since she had lain on her back on a lawn and gazed at the changing patterns of the clouds? It seemed that she and Bud had only looked up at the vast sky over their farm to try to determine if rain or snow would halt the riding lessons that afternoon or the next morning.

Well, life would be changing now. She made up her mind to notice everything around her. She was already charmed by what she saw. "It's all like the drawings I remember in the fairy tale books I read as a child," she told Jacques enthusiastically. "The stepped roofs, the little farms with hedges separating the meadows, the canals with windmills on their banks." A smile came to her lips, a happy feeling welled in her chest. She felt very young and giddy, on the brink of a new adventure.

Her companion did not fail to notice her change of mood. He pointed out places of interest, briefed her on the historical significance of the canals, answered a hundred eager questions. Ariane was certain he had not been fooled by her changing the subject from her romantic visions to a safer topic. He was only giving her a temporary respite. There was not much a person could hide from a man as sensitive and curious as Jacques, she decided, and the thought almost frightened her. With Bud she had always maintained a secret, private room in the back of her mind, just for herself. Jacques Valbonne might always be able to find the right key to unlock the hidden door.

They turned down a cobblestoned road with pastures on either side, large squares of green dotted with horses boasting rich glossy coats. It was spring, and wildflowers filled the meadows. Green pine needles sparkled in the sun from the stately trees that lined the narrow road built centuries ago for carriages.

Some of the thoroughbreds stopped grazing to watch them, their graceful heads erect, nostrils flared. Willie saw them through his trailer window and whinnied loudly. A dapple-gray mare shook her silky mane and whinnied shrilly in return.

Almost at the end of the road was a large country house

of brown rough-edged stones. Three stories high, and covered with dark green ivy, it had white shutters at the windows. Gardens of riotously colorful tulips and daffodils were in the front, and along the side of the house was a large terrace with balustrades and tall French doors opening on to it.

Slightly farther along the road were the stables. As soon as they stopped, a boy Ariane judged to be about ten years old ran up to them.

"How is the new horse, Jacques? Is he as beautiful as Danielle promised?" The eagerness in his face matched that of his tone.

Ariane was struck by the child's shocking resemblance to Jacques. If Jacques had not told her that he'd never been married, she would have taken him for his son.

"Jacques, who is this lady?" the boy asked anxiously when he saw Ariane. She did not know why her presence would cause him alarm, but it was obvious he was not happy about her being there.

"This is Madame Charles, Pierre. She is the horse's former owner."

"But why is she *here*?" he asked worriedly.

"She wants to see her child settled comfortably in his new nursery." He tousled the boy's hair fondly. "And we are going to show her how pretty is our little town of Bruges before she returns to America."

"Oh," the boy said sullenly, thrusting his small hands in his pockets and looking down at the ground.

"Pierre is my assistant," explained Jacques with a wink to Ariane. "He's also the son of a good friend of mine."

Ariane unlocked the trailer and hooked the lead rope onto Willie's halter, urging him back. Working in unison with her, Jacques caught the rope as soon as the horse had backed out.

"For a lady who is through with horses, you certainly hide it well." He grinned at her.

She smiled back. "It's hard to break old habits." When they walked into the stable, she noticed that every stall was immaculately tended. She'd rarely seen houses kept as clean and tidy. All the horses were carefully blanketed and groomed. Several stuck their heads out to see the new arrival and nickered at Willie.

One stallion became enraged at this incursion into his territory and snorted angrily, throwing himself about in his stall. *"Sois sage,"* Jacques called out sternly. *"Be good."* The horse immediately stopped his ruckus. Ariane noted that her host seemed to have all his horses voice-trained. It was something only the very best trainers could accomplish.

Willie's stall was very large. The thick bedding straw was so fresh that Willie tried to nibble on it before he discovered the much more interesting hay in his feed bin.

"This is quite luxurious. You weren't kidding when you said you were putting him in a nursery," said Ariane.

"We have lullabyes piped in every night, don't we, Pierre?" Jacques jested with the boy.

"Oh, yes." Pierre giggled at the joke. "And we give each horse his own teddy bear to sleep with."

Ariane could see that he idolized Jacques. Had she been much older when she met Bud and followed him around in much the same way, laughing at his jokes, hanging on every word?

"Of course, I was going to have his stall painted in red, white, and blue with stars and stripes to make him feel at home," added Jacques wryly. "I hope this decor suits his taste."

"Oh, yes, this is perfect," she replied quickly. "He absolutely adores Louis Seize!"

"What a relief, madame." Jacques made a bow. "The decorator insisted on the rococo ceiling with cherubs winging their way to heaven, but I was afraid the powder-blue flocked wallpaper would offend his sensibility. That's why I had the molding done in gold."

Unable to continue, they burst into peals of laughter together. Ariane realized how odd was the sound of laughter coming from her. It had been months since she had known its wonderful release.

Pierre stood at the stall door watching them. He tried

to laugh, but he did not understand all the nuances of the jokes. He knew only that they excluded him somehow, and he did not find that funny.

Ariane, however, was too caught up in this farewell to her past life to pay much attention to the boy's discomfort.

"Well, so long, pal." She patted Willie's neck fondly. He nuzzled her affectionately, and she found herself brushing tears from her eyes.

Jacques picked up her change of mood and slipped a friendly arm around her shoulders. "We'll take good care of him, don't worry."

She let herself lean comfortably against him, and they remained that way as they walked out of the stable.

"I forgot to mention that Willie's allergic to peaches," she said, suddenly remembering. "He breaks out in hives. We had to cover him with cold towels one summer to get the bumps down."

"We Belgians are not barbarians when it comes to horses," he chided her gently. "We know how to take care of hives."

"And tell your shoer to watch the walls of his hooves. They're rather narrow, and if he doesn't drive the nail in just right—"

"We have an excellent man, the best in the country."

"And he once had a bog spavin, though it cleared up in a couple of weeks..." She stopped herself when she caught Jacques's knowing eyes on her.

"You're finished with all that, remember?" He placed his strong hands on her shoulders and gazed at her with dizzying intensity. She felt a pleasant warmth invade her body. "It will not be easy to cast it aside, Ariane."

She suddenly knew with a woman's instinct that he wanted to kiss her, insane though it was to kiss someone you had just met in front of a stable in broad daylight. Her chin lifted and her lips parted. She longed for it, too, and she reached toward him, feeling the rough tweed of his jacket. She wondered how his skin felt underneath, imagined the way his muscles curved across his chest. He ran his hands down the silk of her blouse, and she understood that he was wondering about her skin, too. His sultry eyelids dropped, and she could feel him stripping her naked, just as he had stripped away the pretenses of her marriage and her thoughts.

"Que tu es belle, Ariane," he said just above a whisper. And she knew he believed her to be as beautiful as the words and the soft voice that uttered them.

"Maman! Maman!" Pierre's small voice brought them back to earth.

Jacques dropped his hands from her quickly, and for a brief second she thought she detected a trace of guilt in his face as he caught his breath.

A white Mercedes had pulled up in front of the stable, and a blond woman in her early thirties stepped out. Everything about the woman spelled wealth and elegance, that insouciant kind of chic that French women seem able to achieve as easily as spraying on a costly perfume. Ariane was familiar with her American counterparts, the rich bored women who reluctantly drove their spoiled children to riding academies but who rarely stepped out of their cars for fear of soiling their Gucci shoes.

"Maman, Jacques has a new horse. It came all the way from America!"

"How lovely, dear," she said in a low, well-modulated voice. She stood by the car, poised as though in an advertisement, and waited for them to reach her. Ariane suspected that the woman would not deign to come any closer to the stables than was absolutely necessary.

Jacques kissed her in the French style on both cheeks and presented her to Ariane. "This is Pierre's mother, my friend Simone Molinard."

Ariane had been taught the European style of shaking hands with everyone, but she hesitated to extend her hand to Simone. "I apologize," she said in French, "but I have been working with the horse, and I'm afraid my hands are dirty."

"I am used to that," she said with a knowing smile to Jacques, but made no attempt to shake Ariane's hand.

"*Maman*, can we stay for lunch?" asked Pierre hopefully.

"No, my little darling, you must go to your piano lesson, and I must go to have my hair coiffed for tonight. You will be over at eight o'clock, Jacques?"

"Tonight?" he asked with surprise.

"*Alors!* You have known for a week. I have invited Michelle and Juan Carlos to dinner."

"But I cannot possibly go anywhere tonight. I have a new horse in. He may have a difficult time adjusting."

"The horses," she muttered with intense loathing, then eyed Ariane with undisguised suspicion. "I cannot disinvite my friends." Her face flushed under the makeup. "They return to Málaga tomorrow."

He sighed. "Then I will come. But I will not stay very late."

"Jacques, *c'est impossible!*" She began a tirade in French that was too fast for Ariane, who instead watched the way little Pierre followed every syllable of the argument with considerable pain, biting his lower lip nervously. The disagreement seemed to resolve itself quickly enough: Simone was once again kissed on both cheeks, Pierre too, and in moments the white Mercedes drove off down the cobblestoned road.

But as Ariane turned back to Jacques, she sensed that the magic that had existed between them only moments before was lost. In an odd way, she was relieved. In the back of her mind was the fear that she would fall into another relationship with a man who put horses before anything or anyone else. Simone Molinard made it clear that she was used to being pitted against the demanding four-legged creatures, and, despite her wealth and sophistication, had not come out a winner.

Ariane considered the white Mercedes wheeling swiftly onto the main road. It was best to dampen any emotion Jacques Valbonne inspired before it was too late to make a rational decision about the man. Not only would she have the horses for competition, but she would have to face a formidable, sophisticated blonde who had already demonstrated her will to fight for him.

But as Jacques turned his dark green eyes back to her, she felt a tingling sensation in her depths and realized with horror that the chance to make a rational decision about him probably had passed the moment she met him.

Chapter Two

A GIRL APPEARED on the terrace and waved to them. "Ariane! How wonderful to see you here!"

Jacques's younger sister, Danielle, was a spirited girl in her mid-twenties with a crop of curly blond hair and a joyful smattering of freckles.

When getting rid of the animals she and Bud owned, Ariane had hesitated until the last moment to sell Wicked Willie. Then she met Danielle Valbonne, and she knew she had found the right owner for him.

"I am so glad you decided to come to Bruges! I told my brother to ask you. We can make a wonderful time. So you know my crazy brother? He has a sense of humor, very bizarre, eh? Wicked Willie is happy in his new home, do you think?" Danielle spoke rapidly, with a charming French accent. "Ah, the Grande Dame of the White Mercedes was here." She glanced with disdain at the car disappearing along the main road and struck a mock-so-phisticated pose reminiscent of Simone. "'I do not like the dirty horses.'" Danielle pointed her button nose in the air, mimicking Simone's low voice. "'So messy a sport, my dear. Is it not, Jacques? Why you do not take up sailing the little boats, my dear, so much more chic, and you can wear such clean white pants?'"

Jacques tried to keep a straight face, but could not help laughing at her mimicry. "You would do well to imitate some of Simone's finer points, Dany. It might make a lady out of you."

"Bah! If that is a lady, I would rather be a horse and merit her contempt."

"What is this talk?" A white-haired man walked through the French doors leading onto the terrace and came forward to greet them, his hand extended toward Ariane's.

"This is our charming papa," said Danielle. "I never had a chance to introduce you when we were in New York. He was always so busy with his affairs."

Jacques laughed. "You mustn't say 'affairs,' Danielle," he corrected, "or Ariane will have the impression that our father spent an entire business trip chasing after women. 'Affairs' in French means something entirely different than in English."

Monsieur Valbonne seemed a little embarrassed. A distinguished man in a dark, conservative three-piece suit, he was the very picture of European nobility and obviously had clearly defined ideas of what sort of conversation was permissible in front of a lady.

"*Je te demande pardon!*" Danielle said, giggling, ignoring her father's discomfort. "Papa was busy with his *business* affairs. That is correct, *n'est-ce pas*? But I forget that we can speak French. Ariane speaks much better French than I do English."

"*Je suis enchanté, madame.*" Monsieur Valbonne took Ariane's hand warmly, and she was suddenly glad that her French mother had drilled her well in the correct things to say at such a moment. Otherwise, words would have failed her. This was a time when all her best manners were needed. The gracious, elderly man had such a royal bearing that she almost felt a curtsy would be in order.

"What a pity we did not have the occasion to meet in New York," he said politely. "It is a fine thoroughbred my daughter bought from you. I saw the papers. How delighted we are that you should honor us with a visit."

"I'm pleased to be here." She wondered how he had so gallantly managed to switch their roles around to make *her* seem like the visiting princess. Then she remembered her mother telling her that the true nobility would always go out of their way to make a guest feel welcome.

"Je meurs de faim!" Jacques said suddenly.

"You always are to die from hunger," said Danielle, "like a wild animal."

"Yes, permit me to take you in to lunch, Ariane," said Monsieur Valbonne. He walked beside her across the terrace, then paused to let her go first through the French doors leading into the house.

As they entered the dining room, Ariane realized that she had entered a level of society that existed only for the very privileged few. It was an aristocratic life-style graced with crystal chandeliers, ornate ancestral paintings, velvet upholstery, hand-embroidered lace tablecloths, and monogrammed silver napkin rings. Yet even amid the heavy, dark, exquisitely carved furniture, the dining room remained infused with light because of the French windows stretching across the entire length of the room, giving a picturesque view of the gardens, meadows, and graceful trees beyond the house.

Crisply uniformed maids padded softly in to serve the soup, and when that course was finished, Danielle rang a tiny silver bell on the table, and the maids reappeared noiselessly to clear the dishes and bring out the roast.

Ariane, who was accustomed to tuna sandwiches on the kitchen table, was awed by the spectacle unfolding before her eyes. And this was an ordinary meal. What did the Valbonne family do on special occasions? But if she had expected the family to act in a stiffly formal manner to fit their surroundings, she was mistaken. They were lively and affectionate, and they did their best to make her feel at home.

"I am very sorry about your husband," said Monsieur Valbonne with genuine sympathy. "I lost my wife in the same way. I have never been an enthusiastic horseman, though we always had fine horses in our stable. After the accident, I'm afraid I lost all interest in the sport."

Ariane was surprised at the deep contrast between father and son, who on the surface resembled each other in many ways. Monsieur Valbonne was the end result of centuries of civilization, a product of the best schools, the finest cultural traditions, while Jacques seemed to be a throwback to one of the more rugged Valbonne *chevaliers* from whom he was descended, perhaps even one of the Spaniards who fought and conquered the Pays-Bas, an adventurer who lived every moment on the edge of some physical challenge or danger. Even the way he ate his meal, slicing his meat with sure swift strokes, savoring his wine, brought up the image of a more sensual past. He caught her gaze, and a smile flickered in the green depths of his eyes, then disappeared once again as he concentrated on enjoying his meal. Part of what was so attractive about him, she realized, was that he was so intensely alive.

"What are your plans now that you are here in Europe?" asked Monsieur Valbonne politely.

"I haven't any definite plans, though I do want to see my aunt in Paris."

"She is French?"

"Yes, my mother's side of the family is all French."

"But of course, your lovely name and your perfect Parisian accent," he complimented her.

"I'm afraid my French is a little rusty, but I hope it will improve now that I'm here. How is it, Monsieur Valbonne, that you speak English with a British accent?"

"In Belgium, one sends children to England to learn English. I went to boarding school there and Oxford later, then to the London School of Economics. And now my business takes me often to London."

"Yes, Danielle told me a bit about your work," Ariane said.

"Don't get him started," cautioned Danielle.

Her father smiled and winked at her. "I promise not to bore our guest with the details. Unfortunately my children, who both love horses, do not care much for my work. It is very complex, the world of modern finance and investments."

"It sounds fascinating," protested Ariane.

"It does?" He seemed surprised at her enthusiastic assessment.

"It conjures up all sorts of marvelous intrigues with

Arab oil sheikhs and executive jets, Swiss bank accounts and computers transferring huge sums of money in microseconds across continents."

Monsieur Valbonne refilled her glass with wine and gazed at her with new respect. "How refreshing to hear a young woman who keeps an open mind. You see, *ma fille, mon fils,* not everyone finds my work dull." He said this with a fatherly twinkle, but Ariane could see that behind the humor lay some disappointment that his children did not appreciate his work.

"Ah, but you did not tell Ariane about the long lists of numbers on the balance sheets, the suffocating smoke-filled conference rooms where you look out the windows, longing to be outside," said Jacques.

"And you did not mention the boring men with balding heads and balding souls," Danielle joined in. "All that talk of money and markets and gold prices. *Quel ennui!* Oh, the boredom—the only thing exciting about money is spending it. Papa, you must see my Wicked Willie. It is the prettiest investment you have ever made."

Monsieur Valbonne turned to his son. "What do you think of the horse, Jacques?" Ariane could see that he respected his opinion in these matters.

"He's a fine stallion," said Jacques without reservation. "But you spoil Dany by indulging her every whim. We had no need of another stallion. And she will never take care of it. Like every other horse you have bought for her, he will become my responsibility."

"Jacques, tu es méchant!" said Danielle petulantly, and, as she had earlier that day, Ariane thought of schoolchildren teasing one another.

Monsieur Valbonne brushed aside Jacques's remark about spoiling Danielle, but Ariane saw that he was sensitive to the accusation. Politely changing the subject, he turned again to Ariane. "You will be staying with us for a few days?"

"Not here, exactly," she hedged. "I thought I'd get a hotel room in Bruges. I wouldn't want to impose on you."

Jacques looked up from his plate, a smile playing at

the edge of his lips. She knew what he was thinking and suddenly regretted mentioning a hotel. No doubt he would take it as an invitation.

But the older man would not hear of such a thing. "A hotel? But we have guest rooms here. It is no imposition. You must not even consider a hotel."

"Yes, do stay here," urged Danielle. "We'll have Jacques take us to the discos in Knokke-Zoute by the seaside—that is, if he can tear himself away from his beloved Simone."

"Why couldn't Simone go with you?" asked Monsieur Valbonne reasonably.

"Simone muss her perfect hair with dancing? *Quelle horreur!*"

"Dany, do you ever have a kind thing to say about poor Simone?" asked Jacques with slight irritation.

"No. She has been the same cold china doll all the years we have known her. Not even motherhood has made her human."

"Danielle, *je t'en prie!*" said Monsieur Valbonne sternly. "I beg of you—You must keep your opinions about Simone to yourself. One day she may be sitting at this table every day as your sister-in-law."

"That is the day I shall go to the stables and eat with the horses."

Ariane's eyes widened as she listened to what was obviously a much rehashed family dispute. She knew there had been a change in Jacques's attitude toward her when Simone appeared, had felt the tension and the jealousy, but she had not realized that Jacques and Simone were close to marriage. She searched for a clue to Jacques's real feelings, but his face, for the first time since she'd met him, was unreadable, and it seemed as though he was purposely avoiding her eyes.

Monsieur Valbonne returned his attention to Ariane. "Then it is settled: you will stay here with us."

"Oh, really, I . . . I can get a hotel," she repeated, feeling obliged to say it. "Besides, I'd only thought to spend the night here and then catch a train for Paris."

"There is no reason to take a hotel room or a train to Paris. I am flying there tomorrow in my private jet and would be delighted to take you along as a passenger."

Suddenly Jacques was watching her carefully, and it made her reluctant to answer Monsieur Valbonne. But what prevented her from going to Paris the next day? Certainly not Jacques, who was practically engaged to Simone.

"Father, perhaps Ariane would *prefer* to stay in a hotel," Jacques interjected suddenly. Her eyes met his, and she recalled in a rush how it had been when they had nearly kissed in front of the stables.

"But she would be so much more comfortable here," argued his father. "Of course, Ariane, it is your decision. If you prefer, I will make reservations for you. I know the owner of the Hotel Van Eyck. It is very comfortable. But we *do* wish you to be our guest."

Ariane was embarrassed now by the attention she was receiving and was certain that Monsieur Valbonne would be insulted if she refused the invitation to stay in his home. "No, really, I would much rather stay here. I just didn't want to inconvenience you."

"We are honored to have you as our guest," said Monsieur Valbonne. "And I suggest that tonight, in honor of our lovely American guest, we all dine at Le Quai Vert. The canals of Bruges are illuminated at night, and you will have a perfect view."

"No, no," objected Danielle. "If Ariane is only going to be here for one night, she must come disco dancing at the seaside. It is much more exciting. Don't you agree, Jacques? Albert is coming for me tonight and we can all go together, the four of us."

"I have to attend a party at Simone's tonight."

"Ah Simone, *ma chère*," sighed Danielle dramatically, tossing her blond curls. Ariane could see that it was impossible for Danielle to hear Simone's name and not take a kittenish swipe at it. She giggled with delight when both her father and brother gave her an annoyed look.

Ariane found herself rooting for Danielle, even though

it was not her place to take a position on such an intimate family matter. "Then if you cannot tear yourself away from the simmering Simone," Danielle continued, "Ariane and I will go with Albert and she will meet all the handsome young Belgemen."

"Belgemen?" Monsieur Valbonne laughed.

"One says Belgian men," corrected Jacques, suppressing his own smile.

"But one says Englishmen and Frenchmen. Why not Belgemen?" protested Danielle.

"Perhaps Ariane should stay here awhile and teach you correct English," commented Jacques.

"There are Dutchmen and Chinamen and . . ." Danielle was not one to easily concede a battle.

"Please, Ariane, tell her," interrupted Jacques.

"I'm afraid he's right." She laughed. "But it doesn't make any sense that there are no Belgemen."

"No. Tonight you will see that there is such a thing as Belgemen and they will all fall madly in love with you."

"You forget that Ariane is a recent widow," said her father thoughtfully. "Perhaps she does not wish to go dancing just yet."

"Oh! *Je m'excuse!* I am so sorry if I offend your sensibility. It is so difficult to think of you as a widow. You are so young! *Eh bien*, perhaps it is better that you go to dinner with Papa at Le Quai Vert. Otherwise he will be all alone tonight. Papa can be very charming company, you'll see, as long as you keep him from talking about commodities and monetary exchanges."

To tell the truth, Ariane would have preferred to go dancing, but it did seem somewhat tasteless for one in her position. She was no daring Scarlett O'Hara.

Even so, she realized that the pain of her widowhood was finally beginning to recede. That she had, even for a moment, considered dancing or had desired briefly to kiss Jacques, that she could even feel a pang of jealousy toward Simone gave Ariane a pleasant tingling feeling. For months she had so completely given herself over to the finality of Bud's death that her own feelings and impulses had become deadened. And now it was as though someone had touched her shoulder, awakening her from a nightmare. Through the tall French doors she saw a white butterfly alight on a yellow daffodil, then flutter away. Jacques crossed her line of vision, stretching up from the table like a lion. He, too, was looking out the glass door. She remembered what he had said about stuffy conference rooms. They were alike in that way, always wanting to be outside. He opened the door and took a deep breath of the fresh air.

"I think we should take Ariane sightseeing in Bruges this afternoon." Danielle put down her napkin and picked up the silver bell to ring for the maids to clear the table.

"Ah, I would love to, but I am engaged for the afternoon," Monsieur Valbonne smiled apologetically at Ariane.

"Then Jacques and I will take her."

"Dany," said Jacques with some irritation as he turned back from the door, "you have some serious business to attend to this afternoon."

"Business?"

"Papa's prettiest investment has been cooped up in a ship for over a week and needs to be exercised."

"I'll do it tomorrow after Ariane leaves."

Jacques appealed to his father. "I expected this in a few weeks after the novelty wore off, but the very first day?"

Monsieur Valbonne frowned, showing clearly that he disliked the role of disciplinarian with his only, favored daughter, but he agreed with Jacques. "You wanted the horse, Danielle, now you must take some responsibility."

She shrugged with resignation. "Well, Jacques, *you* must take Ariane sightseeing, and do not forget to show her our Lac d'Amour."

"Did I hear correctly—a Lake of Love?" Ariane was sure they were kidding her.

"You'll see." His dark green eyes sent sparks out to her, and she felt her knees go weak. Never in her life, not even with Bud, had a man's glance done that to her.

Had he purposely gotten rid of Danielle so that he could

be alone with her? After all, Willie would not need more
than an hour's exercise. She glanced at Danielle. Was
there a slight smile in her mischievous eyes?"

Chapter Three

As THEY DROVE past the stable, Ariane heard Willie whinnying and thumping his hooves against his stall door. She knew from experience that horses usually had a difficult time adjusting to new surroundings, but the plaintive sound of Willie's cry touched her deeply. "Jacques, I can go down there and calm him," she said tentatively.

He gave her an oblique smile. "Is this the woman who was through with horses forever?"

She tried to smile, but the sound of Willie's voice haunted her. Jacques reached over and patted her hand. "Danielle will be with him in a few minutes, and after some exercise he'll be fine," he assured her. He was right, of course, but it didn't make it any easier.

Again, Ariane was stunned by the sky-filled country around them, a land unlike any she'd seen before—other than in the beautiful paintings of the Flemish masters, of course. Yet not even the picturesque countryside had prepared her for the splendor that was Bruges. As they drove over the Porte Sainte-Croix, one of the four remaining medieval bridges that had been built with thick round towers to protect the entrances of Bruges, Ariane had the distinct feeling she was entering a magical place. A wide canal completely surrounded the city, and other small canals crisscrossed, making it the "Venice of the North."

"One can change anything *inside*, but outside it must remain the same," Jacques explained to her. "You can walk into a building in Bruges and find a modern house or department store. But at least when you are walking the streets, you are seeing exactly what you would have seen if you were walking there in the fifteenth century."

"What a wonderful idea to preserve these old facades!"

"Only when the buildings are as beautiful as these. Bruges during the Middle Ages was one of the most prosperous cities in the world. It was the center of European commerce and banking, art and culture. The artisans and craftsmen here were like no others. It is impossible to see it all in an afternoon. You must go back many times to study the detail. It is not unlike discovering a new friend. The first time you are attracted by an overall pleasing quality. And then as you get to know them better, you see a million things to admire." He was looking at her intently, and his gaze made her so nervous that she studied the facade of a building very closely as the car stopped for a traffic signal.

He was right about the intricacy of the buildings, about the almost unbelievable craftsmanship that had gone into their creation. What had at first glance seemed like a beautiful stone arch over a window was actually a sculptured molding of intricate design. The molding was made of the same brown brick as the building, each brick fitting perfectly into place.

They parked the car near the Grande Place and walked to the Belfry, where a bell concert was in progress. "The tower is nearly a hundred feet tall," said Jacques. "From the top, you can see out over the entire countryside all the way to the North Sea."

"Can we go up there?"

"There isn't time if you want to see the rest of the city."

He showed her the other famous landmarks: the Town Hall, with its elaborately sculptured doorways and towering spires, the Chapel of the Holy Blood.

They had been walking for a few hours when he suddenly took her hand. "I want to show you the most special place in all of Bruges."

"What is it?"

"Gruuthuse. It has some historic significance, but I

can't remember what it is anymore. I discovered it as a boy and come here often. It's a beautiful, peaceful spot."

They walked down narrow streets along tree-lined canals. There were several places she would have liked to linger. At each turn was a sight that lifted the spirit: swans gliding along the canals, the brown brick houses with the intricate stone lacework of their facades reflected in the water.

They had passed under an archway and through a building when they suddenly emerged into a quiet garden. It was flanked by two ancient buildings. And everywhere she looked the buildings and trees were placed so as to be pleasing to the eye. "It's like a cloister—the feeling, I mean."

He seemed pleased at her reaction. "Sit right here, right at the end of the bridge. This is the best view."

Ariane sat down and leaned back against the cool stone building. One could look down at the water gently flowing below the bridge or at the patterns of the beautifully constructed Renaissance buildings across the canal. The architect must have planned that very place and garden as a refuge. Sitting there, Ariane felt completely at peace with the world.

"I discovered this place right after my mother died," Jacques told her softly, his hand resting on her shoulder. "I used to take my bicycle and ride into town from Sainte-Croix. Then I'd lean the bicycle against the wall over there and sit here for hours at a time."

Ariane looked up at him. His green eyes were distant. He was sharing a very quiet, hidden part of himself with her. She reached up and touched his hand. He wrapped his long fingers around hers without looking down at her. He had just given her a precious gift.

She thought of her childhood, her marriage, the horses she had trained. Each memory followed the one before it with the clarity of a slide show, ending with the last one of her and Jacques Valbonne hand in hand together on the Pont Saint-Boniface. In some odd, unexplainable way, she felt as though every experience she had ever had had led her to this moment, as though it were the culmination, the sum total of everything she was or ever would be.

"Well, come on," Jacques broke into her thoughts. "We'd better get to the Lac d'Amour before nightfall or Danielle will never forgive me."

"I wouldn't mind skipping it if we could stay here."

He smiled at her and pulled her up to face him. "I'm glad you like it here. Something told me you would."

"It affected me strangely," she admitted. "I could think about things that would ordinarily make me sad and see them—not without emotion—but, how can I say it. . . ."

"Peacefully."

"Yes."

He nodded. "It is the only place where I found I could go over my memories of my mother without feeling the pain of loss."

They walked in silence for a few moments, then Ariane had a sudden, sinking revelation. She stopped and turned to face him directly. "Jacques, why did everything suddenly stop here in the fifteenth century? You told me Bruges was the rival of Florence and Venice, richer than Paris and London. Why didn't it continue to grow?"

A look in his eyes told her that he'd been waiting for her to ask this question, and though it suddenly took on a deeper meaning than she had first realized, he answered matter-of-factly. "The river silted up; the ocean receded from her doorstep. It became impossible to bring the ships in, and so Bruges simply settled into itself and went to sleep."

She almost could not accept the city's fate. Just having spent the morning surrounded by the beauty of the Belgian city made her feel a part of it.

"It must have panicked the inhabitants at that time. Couldn't they do anything to stop it?"

"They tried, but it would have taken modern-day engineering to correct the problem."

"It's sad in a way, but if it had been allowed to grow, it might have changed drastically."

"Change is not always bad, Ariane."

"But it would have lost something."

"Maybe not. Paris grows, but it never loses its soul."

The Lake of Love, as she imagined it would be, was lined with thick green trees dipping down to the water's edge, casting shadowy patterns as snowy-white swans glided across.

They could hear the bells of the ancient Belfry tower chiming in the distance as the blue shadows lengthened into dusk. He took her across the bridge. "You must throw a coin in the water and make a wish."

"And what shall I wish for?"

He pulled her close and looked deeply into her eyes. She tilted her head to meet his gaze. Her heart was pounding in her chest, and she felt her own arms stretch around his neck and pull his face down to her. Their lips touched lightly at first, exploring, tasting, their mouths eager, opening. Their thoughts had been shared all day, and now they wished to pour everything into the physical contact of their first kiss, reluctant to let the moment pass—until Ariane felt the hands that had so urgently pulled him to her press against his chest and push him away. He resisted at first, pulling her even more tightly to him, then he relaxed and let her go. She walked away a few steps, shaky and unsure of her balance, afraid to look at him.

"Is it the memory of your husband? Is it my relationship with Simone? Or is it that we have only just met?"

She looked at him with surprise.

"Well?"

"All three, Jacques. I haven't, I mean . . . well, since Bud . . . it's just that . . ."

"And you're afraid to get involved with a man, especially one who seems to have another woman."

"Oh, damn! Will you stop reading my mind. It makes me nervous. I haven't been able to have a private thought since I met you!"

He laughed and slipped an arm around her. It was a friendly gesture that did not threaten her equilibrium. She relaxed. "It's not just Simone, Jacques. I can't see myself falling in love with another guy who is crazy about horses."

"Do those look like horses to you?" He pointed to the swans gliding under the bridge. "Oh, my God. Quick, kiss me again."

"Why?"

"We must kiss while the swans are going under the bridge."

"What on earth for?"

"No time to explain." He pulled her close, and they kissed. It was Jacques this time who ended it, and quite abruptly. He turned her toward the other side of the bridge to watch the two swans as they swam away.

"What do swans have to do with anything?"

"Bruges is full of legends about swans. There was a lawsuit brought against some fishermen in the seventeenth century who tried to do away with them because they ate too many fish. But they lost, for in the thirteenth century the people of Bruges were condemned to care for them as a penance for killing someone."

"What does that have to do with our kissing just then?"

"There is another legend that if we kiss on the bridge while two swans glide beneath, you will become enchanted and will love me forever."

"What about *you*?"

"I'm equally enchanted. But, unfortunately, nothing can ever come of it," he teased.

"How can you be so sure?" she flirted with him.

"Because you will be in Paris tomorrow and will have forgotten all about me."

They turned and headed back toward the Grande Place. "And you will be at Simone's tonight and not giving me a single thought. So much for legends."

"There you are wrong. I would much rather be with you tonight." He had dropped his playful tone.

"But you and Simone are very serious, aren't you?"

He took a deep breath and threw a pebble into the lake. "It's like that, Ariane."

"Like what?"

"Like throwing a stone into the water. First there is one ripple, then another, and on and on."

"You're evading the issue."

He began a smile that told her she was right. "What does it matter? We are two unfortunate, enchanted people who are condemned by the swan spirits of the lake to love each other."

"You toss the word 'love' around as easily as you toss pebbles into the Lake of Love," she teased him. "I think the 'Belgemen' have been badly underestimated by the world. You are the true romantics, not the Latins." The way he had looked at her earlier at the dining table came back to her, and she laughed. "Is that why you wanted me to stay at a hotel? So you could slip away early from Simone's and..."

"You knew I wanted you to get a hotel room?"

She nodded.

"How did you know?"

She shrugged. "I sensed it. Just like you pick up all *my* thoughts." She stopped and stared at him. "Do you think we have ESP?"

"I don't believe in that sort of thing."

"Oh, just legends of the Lake?"

"That's fact," he said, laughing. "Legend or no legend, you and I are condemned to love each other. Fight it if you will, but it's true. I don't believe we have ESP. Our understanding comes from being around horses. You learn to communicate without words—unless, of course, you have the good fortune to find a horse who speaks fluent French or English. You learn to know what they're thinking by the texture of their muscles, the width of their eyes, the way their nostrils flare, which way their ears are turned."

"Do my ears turn?"

"No, but your nostrils flare like a thoroughbred's, and your eyes grow to twice their already large size when you're disturbed."

"That still doesn't account for it," she argued. "Bud was extremely sensitive to horses, and yet he never had any idea what was going on in *my* mind. What about Simone?"

"Simone and I have no understanding."

They stared at each other in the growing darkness, and their arms reached out instinctively. Ariane felt the searing warmth invade her body as they pressed together.

"I don't know if I like it," she mumbled as their lips brushed.

"Why not?"

"It's disconcerting to have someone know your thoughts. It makes me feel so vulnerable and naked."

"I would love to see you vulnerable and naked." He moved his lips down her neck, pushing her long auburn hair aside. "I've thought of nothing else all day."

She trembled, realizing that she felt the same way. He glided his fingers up under her blouse and touched the soft skin of her back. "My God, you are beautiful, Ariane. I want to possess you, your body, your thoughts, your fears, your joys. I want to possess your very soul. When we go back to my house, tell my father that you've changed your mind and you've decided to take a hotel room."

Her mind raced. It was insane, foolish. And yet she wanted Jacques at that moment more than she had ever wanted anything in her life. What was the risk in having one passionate night of love? She was not foolish enough to believe all the things he said, certainly not foolish enough to think it would last forever. "Then you will tell Simone the dinner is off?" she heard herself say wildly.

"No, I can't do that. I'll get away early and come to you."

She yanked herself away from him. "I've never believed in a double standard."

"You don't understand about Simone."

"I understand perfectly well. You are unwilling to give up a good thing for an unknown quantity, especially one so fleeting as a woman who will be in Paris tomorrow. If you break the date with Simone tonight, she may not be waiting for your loving embrace tomorrow after I'm gone."

"Come on," he said coolly. "It's getting late."

She felt on fire now, burning with rage. And the strength of her anger confused her. Never before had Ariane suffered the tormenting feelings that jealousy aroused. Bud had never given her any reason. "I'm not worth it, then?" she said under her breath.

"Ariane!" He grabbed her shoulders tightly, almost painfully. "Don't ever say such a thing of yourself! You are worth a thousand dreams. I would fight for your love if I thought I could win it. I have taken horses that were believed to be untrainable and turned them into international champions. I do not give up easily. But we have met at a bad time in your life. You are not ready for what I could give you, for what we could be to each other. And no matter what I could say, you would not believe me. You must learn for yourself. You do not trust your own intuition with people the way you do when you're dealing with horses."

Ariane was surprised by his intensity, but the years she had spent with Bud discussing snaffle bits and saddles, oats and alfalfa had left her singularly insensitive to the passionate language of love. While another girl with her lack of experience might have been taken in, Ariane was not swayed so easily. "If I listened to my intuition, I would probably give myself to you in a minute," she said, steadily gazing into his eyes, "but nowhere in that pretty speech did I hear you say that you were willing to break your date with Simone."

"You have a very astute mind." He smiled at her with admiration. "But I meant every word I said."

She laughed. "Words are easy. I have heard trainers who claimed they could bring a horse to capriole, but when you saw them in the ring, they couldn't bring a horse to a trot. It is actions that count."

"You are very right and very beautiful." He leaned down and brushed her cheek with his lips; but she knew he was not going to compromise. Whatever hold Simone Molinard had on him, it would not be broken easily, if at all.

Chapter Four

ARIANE WASN'T SURE what to wear for dinner. The elegance of Bruges belonged to another century. She could not imagine that a restaurant there would require anything formal, and yet one certainly couldn't wear slacks with someone like Monsieur Valbonne.

She decided to ask Danielle, who was dressing for her evening of disco dancing in a hot-pink sequined top and faded denims.

"For Le Quai Vert, something simple, a robe perhaps."

"A robe?"

"Oh no!" Danielle giggled. "My French and my English get so mixed up. A *dress*, you say. Oh, I wish you were going to be here longer: I would have to learn English."

They went back to Ariane's room, and Danielle selected a dress for her. It was one of the stylish dresses she had bought before leaving New York, a beige wraparound in a soft clinging material. The way it fastened at the waist made the neckline quite low, impossible to wear a bra with, and she knew she would have to be careful about leaning over too far. But it had billowy sleeves and a wide sash belt. "You look very chic," Danielle commented, "very French. I saw a dress like this last time I was in Paris and wanted to buy it, but *hélas*! For me, with a short waist and legs too long and not enough up here, it looked very silly. Jacques's girl friend in Paris had one in red, but she was built like you, with the long neck and long waist, and could wear it very beautifully."

Ariane could no longer concentrate on the dress.

"Jacques has a girl friend in Paris—besides Simone?"

"It was a Russian girl in Paris, not very serious for him, I think. And it is no more a love."

"Because he is in love with Simone?"

"*Oh la la!* Please do not say such a vulgar thing. Have pity on me—to have such a sister-in-law!"

Ariane would have liked to ask several more questions but a maid was at the door informing Danielle that her date had arrived to take her dancing.

"Have a nice time tonight," the young woman said cheerily, then kissed Ariane on both cheeks and rushed out the door.

Ariane spun around in front of the mirror. It was a very French-looking dress, all right. She piled her hair on top of her head, swooping it away from her face as she had seen it in a fashion magazine, letting only a few wisps curl delicately over her small ears. Then she rummaged through her suitcase for a pair of panty hose. With horror she realized that she had forgotten to pack any. Ordinarily, it would have given her no cause for alarm, but to dine with Monsieur Valbonne without stockings . . . Her mother's reproving voice echoed in the back of her mind. Danielle had already left, so she could not ask to borrow a pair. She smoothed some lotion over her legs, making them look sleek. Perhaps he wouldn't notice, or he would think it a quaint American custom to go without stockings. He was certainly too much of a gentleman to mention it. She laughed at her concern, attributing it to her strict mother's early training. Monsieur Valbonne was a formal, elderly man who probably would not even think it proper to look at a girl's legs. His son Jacques was another story. It was just as well he was dining elsewhere. Not only would he have noticed, but she was certain he would have embarrassed her with a comment.

Her hair and makeup in place, Ariane walked down the hall in search of the stairs to the main hallway, where she was to meet Monsieur Valbonne. But it was a large house with several connecting halls, and she was soon wandering through an unfamiliar wing. Each time she turned she seemed to be more lost. Rounding a corner, she saw a narrow spiral stairway; it was obviously meant only for the servants' use, but it would at least lead her to the ground floor, where she could find her way more easily.

The stairway was dimly lit and the steps were narrow, making it difficult for her to maneuver in high heels. She inched her way down carefully, for there was not even a rail to hold on to. Suddenly she heard the heavy footsteps of a man bounding up from the floor below. She stopped. It would be impossible to pass someone comfortably in such a narrow space, and she was too far down the stairs to back up to the landing.

Without warning, two masculine hands grabbed her ankles. Ariane gasped, then heard Jacques's hearty laugh.

Relieved, she laughed, too. "Thank heaven, it's you. I was wandering down the hall and took a wrong turn."

"But how fortunate for me. I would never have expected to find such a beautiful pair of legs waiting for me here." He moved his large hands up to the calves of her legs and caressed them. "Very beautiful, indeed!"

"All right, Jacques, now you've had a nice little thrill, let me pass."

He moved up a few stairs, and as he did he slid his hands up her thighs. "What a shame more girls don't consider going without stockings. But then not every girl has lovely slender legs like these."

"Jacques, let go." She was trying to sound cool and authoritative, but her throat was dry and she was trembling involuntarily. Reaching down, she tried to make him release his hands. "Jacques, please!"

He ignored her and laughed when she locked her knees together. She knew his strong hands could easily pull them apart, and she was suddenly angry at his presumption that she was willing to play this game. His thumbs were making small, tantalizing circles on the soft vulnerable skin at the backs of her knees.

"I'm glad you find this so amusing," she said shakily, attempting again to remove his insolent hands.

He moved up and stood at eye level with her, then with one swift motion he released the sash of her dress, and it fell open. "Only the French know how to design dresses for women."

"Yes, devilishly clever, those French." She pulled her dress back around her. "Now, if you'll excuse me..." She felt a surge of anger but was aware that it came from her knowledge of the Russian girl in Paris with the same kind of dress, not just the audacity he displayed in undoing the sash.

"You're not really angry, are you?" He was tying the sash for her, since her hands were trembling. "There, now you look as beautifully untouched as when I encountered you here."

"So glad to have provided some predinner amusement for you."

"I admit it was a game, but I cannot believe that you had no enjoyment."

"None at all." She looked away from him, but he tilted her face back so that she was forced to look into his green eyes. He was suppressing a smile.

"Then I will apologize to you, *chère* Ariane. It was an honest mistake. I felt you shudder, and I thought it was with pleasure, not with anger."

She brushed past him and quickly made it to the bottom of the stairwell without looking back at him. Under different circumstances, she would have admitted that in those few minutes she had experienced the most intense pleasure of her life.

As lovely as Bruges was in the daytime, it was a veritable fairyland at night. The main canals were illuminated, the lights reflecting onto the water. In the darkness, with the damp air coming down off the North Sea, one could easily sustain the illusion of being part of Flemish Renaissance life.

Even the restaurant had been there for at least three centuries. It was small and quaint, with tall windows that looked out over the Quai Vert canal. They were ushered to the table with the best view, the waiters seeming genuinely happy to see Monsieur Valbonne.

It was the kind of candlelit dream restaurant that had run through Ariane's fantasies, and she found herself wishing that Jacques was sitting across from her instead of his father.

"So where did Jacques take you this afternoon?" asked Monsieur Valbonne politely after he had ordered the wine.

To the moon, she was tempted to reply, but instead said, "We saw the Belfry, a beautiful cathedral, and a place with a strange name, the Grut something."

"Ah, the Gruuthuse. Wonderful history attached to that house."

"Jacques didn't tell me any of the history," she said with surprise. To him it had been a personal refuge, and it hadn't occurred to her that it existed for any reason other than Jacques's own emotional needs.

"I should have guessed. Jacques is not much interested in history. He lives entirely in the present. He loves the town for what it is, not what it was. For me, it is the history which is fascinating. Gruuthuse was begun in 1420 by Jan van der Aa and then finished in 1465 by Louis de Bruges, Lord of Gruuthuse, Knight of the Golden Fleece. He was quite a character in his day, even gave asylum to King Henry IV of England. There was actually a skeleton discovered in a secret room that was hidden in back of a chimney in the kitchen."

"Do they know whose it was?"

"There is always speculation, but the identity is a mystery. The house is full of underground secret passageways and hidden stairways."

Ariane thought of Jacques's comment about looking closely at the buildings of Bruges. How many secrets they must contain. She was not sure now if she would have enjoyed the spot as a quiet refuge had she looked at the lovely building and wondered if there were skeletons encased in the secret passageways.

"Jacques is like his mother in that way," Monsieur Valbonne went on. "She used to bicycle all around Bruges and the countryside and ride crazy horses. She enjoyed every moment as it arrived, never dwelt on the past. She was good for me. I tend to overintellectualize everything. She could look at a tulip and see the intrinsic beauty, and I would be more concerned about which variety it was."

"You must miss her very much."

He took another sip of wine and looked out the window over the canal. "Very much."

"Is that why you have never remarried?"

"No. It was because of the children. The way I am traveling, I had little enough of myself to give them. I did not want them to feel they had to compete with another woman. Besides, Jacques and Danielle are both headstrong and opinionated. They would never have accepted another mother. The resentment would have become unbearable."

Ariane was surprised that Monsieur Valbonne was willing to reveal so much of himself. "Yes, I can see how that would happen. I'm fortunate as a widow that I had no children. It must have been very difficult for you to raise them alone."

"And with two such children!" he said, laughing. "Their mother had made them very independent, insisted they develop minds of their own. Jacques at least was old enough to have developed a sense of responsibility, but Danielle..." He gave a helpless gesture. "She is a wonderful, lively girl, but I'm afraid I've spoiled her. It's always been hard for me to say no to her. She leads a somewhat aimless life. It's my fault. Jacques is right. I indulge her too much."

"Would you have liked for Jacques to go into business with you?" She began to wonder how it was that Monsieur Valbonne moved in the world of finance and Jacques seemed only to be concerned with his horses.

"My wife and I felt strongly that children should make of their lives what they choose, not what their parents wish for them. My own father came from the tradition where a gentleman did not work for a living. Money, he felt, came to you as a birthright with a family name. It was my idea to go to London to enter the world of international finance. But just because it is what gives me pleasure is no reason my son should wish it. I respect the work he does. He has won every international prize he has ever worked for, and he makes a good living doing what he loves."

Since Monsieur Valbonne seemed to enjoy talking about his children, Ariane decided to see how much he was willing to reveal about his son's relationship with Simone. "You mentioned at lunch today that Jacques and Simone will be getting married soon. . . ."

"Not if Danielle has her say!" he said, chuckling. "Simone is a very nice girl. We have been friends with her family for years, for many generations. They do not live very far away. Jacques was infatuated with her from the time he could walk. They were always together. We all assumed they would be married when they were old enough. But Jacques surprised us one day and announced he would not marry her, insisting he could not marry a girl who despised horses. I thought it was very frivolous. After all, my wife's passion for horses never interfered with her love for me. Simone was heartbroken and quite angry, as you can imagine after all those years. Her parents took her to the Côte d'Azur to recover from the shock, and within four weeks she had met and married a young Frenchman from a Paris banking family I know quite well."

"Not a young man, I take it, who liked horses."

"No, but if Simone had ordered a husband from a computer service she could not have picked a man who looked any more like Jacques."

"That explains Pierre," said Ariane, inwardly surprised at the tremendous relief she experienced upon hearing the news. "When I first saw him, I thought for sure he was Jacques's son—the resemblance was uncanny."

Monsieur Valbonne gave a bemused half smile. "The child arrived eight months after the wedding—'premature,' of course." There was a slight hint of sarcasm.

She gasped. "Then you think Pierre *is* Jacques's son?"

"Let us say that it is not impossible. Jacques has never

discussed it with me, and it is not my business to pry. But even if it were not so, she did seem happily married for over ten years. Then a few months ago, she came back home with Pierre and announced that she was getting a divorce. She quickly picked up with Jacques again, and they seem to be as much in love as ever. He is with her every day and is very attached to little Pierre. The poor child misses his own father, and Jacques, I suppose, has become a replacement for him."

"Where is Simone's husband?"

"In Paris. He evidently calls Simone every day, sometimes two or three times a day, but she refuses to talk to him. It is very hard on Pierre. I do not understand how parents can do this to their children. Why must they suffer for their parents' childish behavior?"

"And you think Jacques will marry Simone when her divorce is final?" Her heart was pounding as she asked the question, not certain she wanted to hear the reply.

"I am certain of it. I do not think Jacques ever stopped loving Simone, or he would have married someone else. I'm sure now he sees the folly in expecting someone to share his love of horses. Enjoying horses is not like enjoying music, for example."

Ariane felt crushed by Monsieur Valbonne's certainty. The only consoling thought was that she would be in Paris the next day, and with any luck, in the rush of new sights and experiences, Jacques Valbonne would fade quickly from her memory.

When they arrived home, Jacques's car was already in the driveway, and there was a light on at the stable. "Every night he checks on his horses, 'puts them to bed,' we say," Monsieur Valbonne said, laughing.

Ariane could still hear Wicked Willie making a fuss down at the stable. It would probably be a few days before he calmed down completely. She thought about walking down there, then reconsidered. Willie had to adjust on his own, and she was not ready to face Jacques again in so isolated a situation.

Monsieur Valbonne wished her "*Bonne nuit*" and re-
tired to his room after telling her what time his driver
would take them to the airport in the morning.

She went up to undress for bed. The pleasant, high-
ceilinged bedroom had been built before the age of closets
and had a huge mirrored armoire at one end, a green
overstuffed comfortable chair, and a sink and bidet in the
corner. The toilet was in a tiny room down the hall, the
bathtub in another room altogether. She was certain the
indoor plumbing had been added long after the ancient
house had been constructed.

The large four-poster bed appeared to be lumpy, but
once she climbed in she discovered that it was of a very
soft texture and molded itself to her body as though it had
been stuffed with fluffy clouds.

Willie's whinnying could still be heard through the
window in her room, which faced the back of the house.
"Good night, Willie," she whispered. "This is the last
night we'll be together."

How long she had been asleep, she did not know, but
sometime during the night she heard a commotion outside
and woke with a start. From the window she could see
the lights at the stable and spotlights shining from the
house down onto the path. Jacques was coming up from
the stable, and Danielle, in her pink sequined top, was
alighting from a red sports car with her boyfriend. Monsieur Valbonne, in his bathrobe, was standing on the terrace just below her. She opened the window and yelled
down to find out what was happening.

"It is Wicked Willie," said Danielle in a panicked voice.
"He broke down his stall door and got loose."

Ariane rummaged through her suitcase and found a pair
of jeans, then threw on a T-shirt and rushed downstairs.

"Where'd he go?" she asked Jacques, who was coming
out of the house with a large flashlight.

"He jumped the hedges into the meadow."

"Why not just leave him there?" asked Monsieur Valbonne.

"For one thing, the meadow is full of mares, a few of them in season."

"In that case he will have a good welcoming party to Bruges," Danielle said, giggling. Ariane could see that she was a little tipsy.

"But he could also jump the far hedges, land out on the main road, and get hit by a car," said Jacques. "I've got to see if I can get him back."

"Let me help," said Ariane. "I have him voice-trained. I know he'll come to me if I call."

"No. Don't be crazy. I can't let you go out there with a stallion running amok in a herd of mares! You'll get trampled."

"I have a better chance of getting him than you," she said. Her voice was firm, her bearing determined.

Monsieur Valbonne trusted the judgment of his son in handling the problem, but he made his concern for his guest clear. "Ariane, I know you will do what you must, but please be careful," he cautioned. He touched her lightly on the arm, then returned to the house. It was, after all, the middle of the night.

Jacques started out toward the meadow, and Ariane went after him. "Ariane, don't go. It's dangerous," Danielle called after her, but she ignored the warning. "If you go, I will go, too. He is my horse."

At that, Jacques wheeled around and grabbed his sister's arm. "What Ariane does is her own business, but you are mine. You've been drinking at the discos, and while you may be able to dance up a storm, you're having trouble putting one foot in front of the other just to walk. You'll be no help out there in the dark. Go to bed. There will be plenty of work to do tomorrow."

Danielle was obviously relieved at having been ordered to do what she wanted to do anyway, and she made only a slight pretense of being reluctant to leave them.

Jacques and Ariane dashed outside and down to the meadow. They were only a few feet inside the meadow gate when it began to drizzle. By the time they had trudged halfway across the field, they found themselves in the middle of a harsh pounding rain, which soaked Ariane's thin T-shirt. Jacques's shirt, thrown on in a hurry, was not even buttoned, and in the pale light she could see the rain glistening on his skin. His black hair hung matted over eyes, which burned with anger. "Damn horse," he muttered.

"If you were a stallion and knew there was a whole meadow of willing mares outside, you'd have probably done the same thing," she said.

He laughed, her remark having broken the tension they both felt. "You're probably right. If there is a filly out of this I shall name her Ariane in your honor."

"You'd be very lucky. He produces beautiful babies."

"Well, let's hope we don't find him out there in the process of making one or we're in big trouble."

They were sloshing through mud puddles now. Her shoes were soaked straight through, and the rain made her jeans cling heavily to her legs. Not far away they could see some horses standing under the shelter of a tree. "You wait here. I'll go up and see if he's with them," said Jacques.

"Let me try to call first, if he's there, he'll come to me."

"You are sure he'll leave six gorgeous thoroughbred mares and come to *you*?"

"Let's see. Willie!" she shouted. "Get over here, you Wicked Willie!"

They could see some of the horses stir in the shadows, but none of them moved.

"Come on, Willie, get over here!"

One of the horses snorted and moved out from the rest to get a better look at who was coming. Jacques shined the flashlight. It wasn't Willie. "I don't think your baby is with them. They're too calm to be harboring a fugitive stallion in their midst."

He and Ariane walked up to them and satisfied themselves that Willie wasn't among them. Just then they saw the outline of a thoroughbred racing across the meadow like a madman on a rampage. "That's the kid," she said.

Even through the rain, they could see the outline of his graceful movements against the gray-black sky.

"He moves like a dream," said Jacques with genuine admiration.

Ariane felt a pang of regret in the back of her throat. She remembered the first time she had seen him run as a colt, flying across the fields of her farm at his mother's side. She knew then he would be something special.

"Willie!" she shouted at him. "Come over here, Willie, you Wicked Willie!"

He stopped and lifted his head very high, looking in the direction of the sound, pricking his ears.

"Come on, Willie. Get over here."

He took a few tentative steps toward them, then stopped and shook out his long red mane. "I don't think the prodigal son wants to come home just yet," mused Jacques.

"He doesn't care for the rain. Being wet might change his mind. Willie!"

The animal stopped to listen and began walking toward them. "Just stay still," she cautioned Jacques. "If we come at him he may turn and run."

They waited calmly, almost holding their breath until the thoroughbred reached them. Willie did seem glad to see Ariane, nuzzling his head against her. They easily slipped the halter they had brought on him and led him quietly back to the stable.

"I have to hand it to you," said Jacques with admiration. "It is not easy to get a stallion voice-trained like that."

"It takes a lot of patience, but it sure pays off in the long run."

"That's why I like to start them off as colts," said Jacques. "Then they know you and are more anxious to cooperate. You've got to be constantly with them from the moment they're born."

Ariane nodded in agreement. "That's what I did with Willie. You can work around him, touch him anywhere."

They talked about methods of training colts all the way back across the meadow, forgetting about the rain and the mud and the danger they'd shared. She was surprised to learn that many of their methods were identical.

"The basic thing, I think, is to give them a lot of love but be stern with them," said Ariane.

"I've never agreed with these trainers who try to instill fear in a horse," agreed Jacques. "They've got to respect you, yes, but if they're afraid, one day they'll turn on you. It never fails."

They worked in unison drying Willie with towels. It was important to make sure he didn't catch a chill. The horses in the field could stand against each other for warmth or move around, but a horse could not be left damp in a stall. When they were through, Ariane brushed him while Jacques cleaned the mud out of his hooves with a hoof pick.

They chatted easily as they worked, several times inadvertently brushing up against each other. Both of them were sopping wet, their shirts and pants clinging to their bodies. Ariane could not help but notice Jacques's hard, muscled chest covered with dark hair matted from the rain. She was aware that his black-fringed green eyes moved over her body, too, watching the way her thin shirt clung to her breasts, the cold dampness making her nipples stand out. There was a sensuousness in rubbing the horse, and though they both noticed he had been with a mare, they said nothing. What should have been a most natural topic between professional horse trainers became suddenly taboo. Jacques cleaned the horse off but did not say a word about his obvious condition.

When there was nothing more to be done, they blanketed Willie and went to fetch him some more hay. Ariane followed Jacques into the large feed room. The fresh scent of the spring hay was like an intoxicating perfume. But before Jacques switched on the light he pulled her close.

Their hair and faces were wet and tasted like rain. She had not realized how cold she was until her body pressed against his and felt his overwhelming warmth enclose her. She let her lips slide down his strong throat and taste the delicious skin there, slightly brittle in the places where he shaved. His lips searched hers, licking, tasting, his tongue plunging into her hungry mouth. She drew him into her with her own lips, grasping the straining muscles of his back, the taut skin under his damp shirt.

He slid his long fingers under her shirt and took a breast in his hands, gently twisting the nipple already hardened from the rain and now excited by his touch. In a deft, swift move he lifted her shirt above her breasts and moved his mouth down on them.

She gasped and trembled as they slipped down onto the hay. Nothing mattered anymore, no memories, no decorum. Only the raging moment. She experienced the feeling of racing over fields on the back of a wild stallion in the wind. She felt his strong leg drop between hers, forcing her thighs apart. He was working the zipper on her jeans. "No, Jacques," she whispered, trying to regain some of her willpower.

"Oh, God, *yes*, Ariane."

She yanked herself up and tried to breathe evenly, pulling down her shirt. "Please, Jacques, I . . ." She closed her lips tightly and tried to hold back the tears.

"You're not ready yet for love," he said with a gentleness that surprised her, following so swiftly on the heels of his violent passion of a few moments before. "I wish you were staying here longer. Like a frightened filly, I could make you forget the past. We would go slowly, a little at a time . . ."

"Until I became your pet, doing exactly as you said? You think you can train a woman like you train a horse?" she asked with bitter amusement. "Perhaps you think you could voice-train me, too?"

He held her close, but without the demanding, frantic sexual power of a few moments before. "Beautiful Ariane." He stroked her thick auburn hair. "Are we so different from the animals we love?"

He stood up and gave her a hand to help her up. They took the hay to Willie, and Ariane kissed the horse on the nose. "Willie, you are going to have to behave yourself better from now on."

He nickered at her as they walked out. "The sun's coming up." She looked around her with surprise. It had stopped raining, and the sky, though still heavy with low, gray clouds, was showing patches of hazy blue. They breathed in the morning air. "A good time to go riding," said Jacques, opening his eyes wide as though to trap all the morning light in their green depths.

"I don't know about you, but I'm going to bed."

"That's right. You go to Paris tomorrow. . . . I mean, today."

She was hoping he would suggest she stay there again, but he walked with her in silence to the house. "*Bon voyage.*" He gave her a crooked smile.

"Jacques?" She reached out and caught his hand.

He pulled her close. "Ariane," he said huskily, "don't leave."

The fear washed over her as she gazed into his eyes. It was a fear she knew she had experienced before. It was like the feeling that had struck her when she first tried to mount a horse after Bud's accident.

Chapter Five

DANIELLE WAS AT the door to her room. "Papa's driver is here, Ariane. I know you were up all night. Are you sure you want to leave this morning?"

"Yes. It will just take me a moment to pack my suitcase and get ready. Can he wait?"

Danielle yawned and shrugged. "That is the advantage of having a private jet. It *must* wait for you."

Just the same, Ariane hurried to put her things on. Her long hair, as always after she had been caught in the rain, was impossible to manage. She pulled it back tightly, the way she used to do before horse shows, and slipped a ribbon around it, gathering it at the nape of her neck. The style was tidy and not unbecoming. She had soft but very definite features, and the severe look accented her large eyes.

Jacques was sitting at the dining room table dressed in his long boots and a clean shirt open at the neck. Remembering how that strong throat had felt under her lips the night before made her tremble. She tried not to look at him.

Monsieur Valbonne, looking fresh and ready for work in a handsome suit, entered the room. "Please take your time, Ariane. There is no rush. Enjoy some *tartines* and coffee before we go. Excuse me, but I must get some papers together."

Jacques was buttering the long slices of Flemish bread and spreading them with raspberry confiture. A maid poured half a cup of coffee, filled the rest with steaming hot milk, and served the café au lait to Ariane. She took some of the delicious bread, still trying to avoid Jacques's green eyes, which were staring at her.

"Have you been down to the horses yet this morning?" she asked at last, attempting to relieve the tension with conversation.

"I never went to bed. I went riding after I left you, then came back here for breakfast."

"Has Willie recovered from his midnight jaunt through the meadow?"

"I was debating whether or not to tell you," he said with concern.

"Tell me what?" She looked up at him, startled.

"His hocks are swollen. Did you say he once had a bog spavin?"

"Last year. We had worked him too hard just before an important show. Oh, no, do you think he's got it again?"

Jacques nodded. "I'm going to call the vet right after breakfast."

"But the vet will just shoot him with cortisone. It's very painful."

"He's in pain right now. I can't see letting him suffer."

"There's no reason to. Bud and I discovered some great stuff. It's just some chemicals mixed together that you can apply to the surface that takes the swelling down. It's not dangerous."

"Chemicals that you apply? I've never heard of such a thing."

"It's very easy to do, and I could make it up for you if you can get me the chemicals."

"How often do you apply it?"

"A few times a day for a week or two. There's a special way to wrap the legs up. I could show you."

"I don't know," said Jacques thoughtfully. "The cortisone shots would be easier."

"For you maybe," she said with irritation, "but not for Willie."

Jacques's father entered the dining room. It was obvious he was anxious to be on his way.

"Monsieur Valbonne, I'm very sorry to keep you waiting, but Jacques has just told me that Willie developed a bog spavin," she informed the older man, both her voice and her eyes conveying her concern about the animal she had so recently relinquished to them.

"That is a very serious ailment for a horse, but you must not worry," he told her in a comforting tone. "Jacques knows all the best methods of taking care of horses. He is probably more expert than the veterinarians."

"In this instance, I may not be," said Jacques. "Ariane has just told me about a new method for treating bog spavin." He turned back to Ariane. "I know you are anxious to go to Paris, but I would appreciate your showing me your chemicals."

She breathed easier at his words. At least he was willing to try something new. She shuddered at the thought of Wille having to endure the painful cortisone shots. "You were very kind to offer to fly me to Paris, Monsieur Valbonne," she apologized, "and I hope I did not hold you up."

"It was no trouble; please do not be concerned. If I can be of any help to you while you are in Paris, please leave a message at my office." He extended his hand to her. "I am so glad I had a chance to meet the charming lady my daughter spoke so highly of. We are honored to have you as a guest. Please consider this your home whenever you are in Bruges."

As soon as Monsieur Valbonne left the room, she and Jacques returned to their conversation about Willie.

"Does he seem to be favoring any one of his feet?" she asked him.

"The left hind leg."

"That's where he had it the worst last time. Let me get changed and then let's go have a look at him. I'll be right back," she said as she walked toward the stairs.

After she came downstairs again she accompanied

Jacques to the stable to see Willie. "Bog spavin, all right, you silly Willie," she said after looking at his leg.

"You should have told your baby that chasing the girls in the middle of the night would get him in trouble," said Jacques.

Ariane wrote down which chemicals to buy and in what quantities. "At first Bud and I used to buy it already made from the vet. But we found it was cheaper to make it ourselves. We used to make our own fly wipe, mix our own feeds. You'd be surprised at the money you can save by doing these things yourself."

When he returned with the ingredients, she made up the mixture and applied it, then wrapped Willie's legs. "That should draw out the fluid."

"I'm fascinated by this," said Jacques. "If for no other reason, I'm glad you showed up because I've learned something very useful to me."

Danielle had gone back to bed after waking Ariane, but now she was up and in her riding clothes. "You're still here!" she shouted with joy. *"Merveilleux!"* But when Jacques told her the reason for Ariane's staying, her spirits dampened. "And I so wanted to show you how beautiful he is to ride today, Jacques. A horse like this you have never seen before. I exercised him yesterday afternoon, and he glides like a swan."

"I had a chance to see him in motion last night," he said. "And he was beautiful. You made a good buy."

"So you at last have faith in my judgment," she said, smiling. Then with mischief she asked, "How was your dinner last night with Simone?"

"She made her famous *côtes de porc à l'antillaise.*"

"How apt," said Danielle dryly. "Simone *is* a side of pork."

Jacques cuffed her playfully. "Simone likes *you*, you know."

"There is nothing sadder than unrequited love, eh, Ariane?" Danielle said laughingly, then deftly changed the subject. "Ah, but I am happy. Now Ariane will have a chance to see more of Bruges and the countryside. What

do you say we go to Ostend tonight? Jacques will be with
Simone again, I'm sure, but there is a cocktail party on
a ship of the Dutch navy."

"What are you doing with the Dutch navy?" asked
Jacques.

"You make it sound so slimy, Jacques!" She tossed her
blond curls. "You remember Christiaan, the tall blond
demigod I was in love with last summer."

"One would have to be a computer to keep track of all
your loves," Jacques said, laughing.

"Christiaan was the officer in the Dutch navy," she
said, ignoring his gibe. "You liked him, remember? Even
Papa thought he had a brain, which is a big compliment
from Papa. Well, I saw him at the yacht club in Zeebrugge
last night, and he invited me tonight. That is something
respectable Ariane, being a widow, could attend, don't
you think? It is not the same thing as disco dancing. And
Ariane, you must see the Dutch seamen—they are all very
handsome."

"Wasn't Popeye a Dutchman?" Jacques teased her.

"Well, if *you* weren't busy with Simone, you could
come with us."

"I have made no plans to be with Simone tonight."

"Excellent! Then we shall all drive to Ostend to the
party," she said gaily. "Perhaps we should surprise them
and all arrive wearing sailor suits. No? Well, if you two
are afraid to offend the Dutch navy, I am not. I must have
a sailor suit somewhere in my room. I'm going to look
for it."

Ariane looked at Jacques after Danielle left. He was
smiling at her. "We have a date, it seems."

She flashed back a smile. "It would have been nicer
if you'd asked me yourself."

"I'm only going along to protect you from the Dutch
navy."

"Can a Belgian horseman stave off the entire Dutch
navy single-handed?"

"I'll give it a try and hope they don't toss me overboard.
You'll be spending another night here, then?"

She gave him a sidelong glance. His strong white teeth and roguish eyes were giving him a savage look that made her knees feel weak. "Just one night more."

Danielle wanted to take Ariane sightseeing again that afternoon, but knowing she would need her strength to face the Dutch navy, Ariane opted instead for a nap. She awoke at sunset feeling rested and started out for the stable to check on Willie. Simone was just arriving in her white Mercedes to pick up Pierre.

"You're still here?" Simone asked her, not trying very hard to mask her annoyance at this unwelcome discovery.

"Last time I checked." Ariane's flippant reply hid her surprise at the rudeness of Simone's question. Was it any wonder Danielle felt the way she did about this woman, she mused.

"Where's Jacques?"

"I don't know. I just woke up."

"You're quite a late sleeper."

"I was up all night." Ariane was so pleased to see the darting suspicion and anger cross Simone's face that she decided not to elaborate. Let Simone think what she would.

"I was just going down to the stable. Shall I tell Jacques you're here?"

"I'll go with you," said Simone quickly, glancing furtively down at her high-heeled sandals. Apparently there was no sacrifice too great to prevent Ariane from having a moment alone with Jacques.

"Hello, *Maman*," called Pierre from one of the stalls. He was doing a creditable job of handling a manure rake that was twice his size.

"Jacques," said Simone with irritation, "I don't understand why Pierre must do this sort of work. Don't you *hire* people to clean stalls?"

"The man who usually does it is home ill with the flu. Even Danielle was down here helping us today. Your son has been doing an excellent job, haven't you, Pierre?"

"I cleaned five stalls all by myself," he said proudly.

Simone shivered with disgust. "I give him piano lessons

and you ruin his hands with this awful business."

"It does not hurt my hands, and Jacques says that it is a good way to build muscles in my arms and back for riding," interjected the boy.

Then he pushed a loaded wheelbarrow out of the stall as Simone stood back in horror, placing her manicured fingers over her delicate, aristocratic nose. "*Mon Dieu*," she whispered.

Jacques leaned his own rake against the wall and came over to them. "Willie isn't much improved," he said to Ariane. "I just took a look at him. I'm still not sure what to do with the wraps so I left them off."

"I'll take care of it," she said, anxious to get away. Simone was giving her an intimidating look that made her feel it would be better to be somewhere else. Willie's stall, however, was not far away, and she could hear their conversation as she worked.

"What time will you be over tonight?" Simone asked Jacques sweetly.

"Uh . . . tonight we have been invited to a dinner at the Dutch navy ship in Ostend."

"Ah, how delightful," Simone purred happily. "I love Ostend. Remember when we used to go dancing there at the *caves*, then walk along the waterfront? What time will you pick me up?"

Ariane's mouth fell open. Simone had simply assumed that the "we" included her. How would Jacques handle her otherwise?

"It is Danielle's old boyfriend who gave us the invitation," he began. Ariane could tell that his voice was troubled. He was searching for the right words.

"Danielle has so many boyfriends," she said, laughing. "For a girl who never pays too much attention to her appearance, she always seems to have a string of them, doesn't she? Well, I must be going if I'm to be ready in time. It's already late. What time will you be by?"

There was a silence. He would have to tell her now, thought Ariane.

"About seven o'clock," she heard him say. So! He

could not even break a date that hadn't been made! Ariane felt betrayed and angry for having deceived herself. And Jacques—he was either two-faced or he did not have the backbone to stand up to Simone. Either way he had tumbled in her estimation.

Ariane noticed that Danielle wasn't informed of Simone's inclusion until just before they started off. And then she flew into a rage. "You coward!" was one of her lesser accusations.

"Look, Dany, Simone is going through a difficult time. I am not going to hurt her feelings simply because you would wish to be rude to her."

"She is playing you mercilessly," Danielle shot back at him. "All the guilt you felt at leaving her ten years ago—she has made a rope out of it and is slowly strangling you with it. Why should *you* feel guilty because her husband threw her out?"

"He didn't throw her out. She left."

"I'd like to hear Jean-Paul's side of the story," she grumbled.

Ariane was feeling more and more uncomfortable. She wished that she had decided to stay home and almost did on the pretext of looking after Willie.

When they picked up Simone later that day, Danielle managed to hide her true feelings and was civil. Her father's training, no doubt, thought Ariane. Simone was the most cheerful one in the car and chattered gaily about Ostend, reminding Jacques of the good times they used to have there. "Do you remember the time my cousin was visiting here from Brussels, the girl you thought was so shy, Danielle?"

Danielle began to laugh. "And after a few drinks, she stood up on the table and began belting out songs like Edith Piaf!"

"And there was that string bean of a fellow who kept following her around all night," said Jacques. "We couldn't get rid of him."

"What a funny night, all of us linking arms and running down the *quais* singing at the top of our lungs," Simone

said, laughing gaily. "How much fun it was to be young
and in love."

Ariane felt even more isolated by their reminiscences.
There was nothing she could contribute to such a conversation. She'd never even had similar experiences at home.
At that age, her main enjoyment had been winning blue
ribbons.

The Ostend harbor was beautiful, with all the ship's
masts lit up like Christmas trees with tiny lights. The smell
of the North Sea borne on a sharp wind was invigorating.
Christiaan, a tall, good-looking blond officer with a trim
mustache, greeted them with immense pleasure. Danielle
had not been exaggerating in her glowing description of
the hearty Dutch sailors, and they seemed to be equally
appreciative of Ariane's good looks.

While Simone clung tightly to Jacques's arm and Christiaan monopolized Danielle, Ariane found herself rela-
tively free to be entertained by several charming Dutch
officers and one American from California serving with
the Dutch on a NATO exchange. She sat among them
during dinner without paying the slightest attention to
Jacques, though once or twice she managed to steal a
glance at him. On those occasions she found that he was
watching her, too, and she quickly turned back to her
attentive officers. He had chosen to bring Simone: let him
live with that. She would be gone the next day. Why
should she lower herself to compete with Simone? In a
way, she even felt sorry for her—a woman so insecure
that she had to cling to Jacques.

It was easy for Ariane to understand why Danielle had
a lot of boyfriends. She was bright and full of fun, always
teasing and flirting in a lighthearted way. True to her
promise, she had found a sort of sailor outfit to wear
featuring a white middy blouse and gathered in with a
wide red leather belt. With her perky, impish looks, she
even managed to make her improvised costume seem like
the latest fashion trend. And it provided the group with
a string of jokes and comments, keeping Danielle at the
center of attention, a role she handled with obvious delight.

Ariane decided that it was Danielle's real indifference to her looks that attracted men. Simone, though much more beautiful, had a cold air of perfection that intimidated them. Constantly preening, she was so standoffish, so worried that every hair was in place, that she could not relax and just have a good time.

"Christiaan suggests we all go dancing in the *caves*," Danielle whispered to Ariane. "They are really discos along the *quais*, under the ground, very *sympathique* ... how do you say in English?"

"Charming, likable—they must be nice."

"Yes, very nice. But if you would not like to go, we will stay here."

Ariane did not want to spoil the others' evening by playing the bereaved widow, so she agreed to go along.

"You are enjoying yourself?" Danielle asked her.

"Oh, yes. This is really good for me, I think, to be out with other young people. I'm glad I stayed over."

"I was angry at my brother at first, but now I see that this was best for you. Here, it is like a buffet dinner. You can take your pick of delicious treats. But Dutchmen are not as *sympathique* as Belgemen—so formal, I think. Ah, but there is a blond Apollo with midnight-blue eyes. He has been looking at you all night. Or the dark-haired one with the mustache. Don't you love mustaches? So masculine. What do you think of Christiaan?" she asked hopefully.

"He seems to be smitten with you," responded Ariane, knowing how important her opinion would be to the young Belgian.

"Smitten?" Danielle repeated the unfamiliar word.

"He *likes* you very much," explained Ariane, to her companion's obvious delight.

Christiaan was approaching them, and Danielle tilted her head up. "Are you smitten with me, my sweetie?" she asked him, a mischievous look on her face.

He laughed. "Wouldn't think of it. What kind of a man do you think I am?"

"I know what kind of man you are. Come on, Popeye, we are going to dance."

They left the Dutch ship in a large group to go to the *caves*. Ariane felt wonderful to be out in the night, the sharp wind tousling her hair, filling her lungs. As it had the night before, a light rain was falling, and she turned her face up to the welcome drops, shaking out her long auburn hair, letting it blow in gusts around her face. Her coat fell open, but she did not feel the cold, partially because of the wine she had had, but mostly because of a gentle warmth that came from within. She was glad to be young and alive, in a new country amidst new friends. She linked arms with the Californian and the Dutch officer while they walked briskly down the *quai*. As she laughed and flirted with them, she caught a brief glimpse of Jacques staring blackly at her. She flashed him a good-natured smile, but he didn't return it.

Poor Simone. The damp sharp winds that were the source of so much joy to Ariane were creating havoc with the elegant woman's coiffure. Trying to keep her style in place with both hands, she huddled over like Eve fleeing the wrath of her Maker.

Danielle, as usual, was clowning. She had put on Christiaan's officer's hat and was singing, "I'm Popeye the Sailor Man," at the top of her lungs while doing, much to his delight, a jig around him. Ariane could not help but admire Danielle, a girl who was so natural, so unaffected, so full of *joie de vivre*.

They entered a door under a neon sign that read La Bamba Café and walked down a flight of twisting stairs. It was one of the many *caves* in Ostend where young people gathered to dance. Though it was not very different from any disco in the States, for Ariane it could have been Katmandu, she had so little experience with this sort of life.

She marveled at the costumes of the dancers, who, like rare birds, had donned their most brightly colored plumage, obviously in hopes of attracting a mate. But amazingly, nobody appeared openly interested in anyone else. The overall expression was of intense boredom. All the excitement was generated by the electric lights flashing on and off on the walls and ceilings and by the hard, driving, crashing music that was electronically timed to one's heartbeat. How, marveled Ariane, could they remain so blasé in the midst of all this raging turmoil?

Yet after the first eye-opening half hour she, too, felt herself becoming numb to the carefully computerized stimulation. Outside in the wind and rain, the brisk salt air, she had felt vibrant, capable of conquering the world. But in the depths of the electronic *cave* she felt washed out, bereft of any human emotions.

The music was so loud that conversation was impossible. One could only dance, and since she did not know the gyrating movements, she stayed at the table on the sidelines and watched. Because Ariane was sitting them out, the American naval officer asked Simone to dance. She reluctantly accepted, only because Jacques insisted on it. He wasn't dancing either.

"Well, how do you like our *caves*?" he asked as he moved over to sit next to Ariane. He had to almost shout to be heard.

She wrinkled her nose. "I always worried that I had missed something in life. Now this is one less thing to worry about. Your sister seems to enjoy it, though. It surprises me. Knowing her the little I do, I wouldn't think she would."

Jacques smiled. "You could place Danielle down in the middle of the Sahara Desert and she would find something there to amuse her. That is her main talent in life. And she loves to dance."

"She moves as if there are no bones in her body!" said Ariane laughingly.

A young man came up to their table with a drink in his hand. Jacques stood up, shook hands with him, and invited him to join them. "Bernard, good to see you here. This is Ariane, a trainer from the States. She just brought us over a beautiful new stallion. You'll see him Monday morning. Bernard is my main trainer," he told Ariane. "We're getting the horses ready for a big show in Brussels next month."

The young man looked down, obviously ill at ease. "I was going to call you, Jacques, then I saw you here and thought, well, I'd talk to you now. I was offered a job at a Paris riding academy. It wasn't the money. They're paying me less than you are, but my girl friend is there, as you know. We're going to be married in a few weeks, and she does not want to be so far away from her family." He shrugged helplessly. "What can I do?"

Though she'd only known him a few days, Ariane could see that Jacques was irritated, but he held his true feelings in check. "You couldn't put it off a month—just until after the horse show? This really is hard time for me to lose you," he said.

"They want me to start the new job next week."

"Couldn't you call them?" Jacques said insistently.

"I already asked and they refused. They need someone right away, and you know these jobs don't come along every day. Our profession is not like being a doctor or lawyer."

Jacques shook hands with him again. "Well, good luck to you, Bernard. If you ever need a recommendation, let me know. You've done an excellent job with my horses."

As soon as Bernard left, Jacques dropped his pretense of cheerfulness. "Damn! I was depending on him. I can always call old Marcel, but then I never know if he's going to be sober or not." He sat lost in thought for a few minutes, then quickly turned to Ariane. "You!"

"Don't look at *me*," she said, realizing immediately what he wanted.

"Just for a few weeks?"

"I told you when we met that I was through with horses. Besides, even if I still planned to be a trainer, I don't think I could . . ." There was a blast of electronic noise from the speakers.

"Think you could what?" Jacques leaned close, as though he believed she had finished her sentence and the words had been drowned by the loud music.

Simone and the American were approaching the table, Simone trying desperately to push a strand of hair back in place and discreetly mop an upper lip that had produced a few distressing beads of perspiration. Ariane turned away from Jacques, ostensibly to welcome the couple back but actually in the hope of ending conversation with Jacques. He, however, would not drop the matter.

"Look, Ariane, this is strictly a job offer."

She sighed. "I know."

"You'd prefer it wasn't just a job offer?" He smiled wickedly at her, and she felt her heart pound.

Simone was now within hearing range and ignoring the American in hopes of catching a bit of the conversation between Jacques and Ariane. The blaring music made it difficult, so she leaned forward.

"Neither offer is even remotely acceptable," said Ariane to Jacques in English, hoping that Simone's grasp of English was as keen as her grasp of horsemanship.

But Simone caught the last two words. "The word 'acceptable'—it is the same in French?"

Ariane nodded.

"But what is the other word, remo...?"

"Remotely. That is *faiblement* in this instance," said Ariane.

"Oh, and *what* is remotely acceptable?" Ariane marveled that it did not bother Simone in the least to be prying into a conversation that was going on before she arrived. Such behavior took a lot of nerve—and a great desire to know.

"Jacques will explain," said Ariane quickly. "I am not sure I could translate it well into French."

Jacques shot her an amused look; she smiled innocently at him.

"Yes, Jacques?" Simone pressed him. She was not deaf to the subtle language of their glances.

"My trainer Bernard was just here. He's going off to

Paris. I offered Ariane his job for a few weeks, and she told me that it was remotely acceptable to her."

Simone nervously pressed her hair into place again and tried to sound pleasant. "I can see why it is only *remotely* acceptable—after all, you are on a vacation, dear. It would not be so amusing for you to work."

"You're absolutely right, Simone. Besides, I told Jacques that I do not wish to train horses for a living anymore."

"I don't blame you," said Simone, visibly relieved at the news. "I cannot imagine a worse profession for a woman."

At that Ariane took offense. Women, she had always believed, made excellent trainers. "Why do you think it is such a bad profession for a woman?"

"The *work* you must do around them! How could you keep your fingernails long or with any polish?" she said with a flutter of her own carefully manicured nails.

Ariane could not take offense at that kind of reasoning and tried to suppress a laugh. Never in her life had she paid any attention to her nails beyond keeping them short and clean. "I cannot argue with you there," she told Simone with a sincere smile.

Feeling magnanimous now, Simone offered, "When you get to Paris, I shall give you the name of a wonderful manicurist named Rosanne in a shop off the Champs Élysées. She is the only person in the world who can do nails. I am going mad here in Belgium, where there is no one who can do a decent manicure. I might as well be living in central Africa. Paris is truly the only civilized city in the world."

Ariane tried to appear politely interested. She had heard the same talk for years from the mothers of the children who came to the riding academy. Were these women's minds devoid of any other concern? Were they nothing more than narcissistic artists whose perennial canvases were their own bodies?

Out of the corner of her eye she could see that Jacques was greatly amused by her show of interest in Simone's fingernail agonies. How could he be in love with a woman like that? Granted, she was the very perfection of beauty, but she wasn't at all the kind of woman he should marry.

What crossed her mind next greatly disturbed her because of the rapidity with which it slid into her consciousness. Since Simone obviously would make Jacques miserable, perhaps she should stay in Belgium for a few weeks if for no other reason than to throw a wrench into the works of that engagement. What a horrid thought! Never had she meddled in anyone's life. And if she did stoop so low as to conspire against them, what role did that leave her? The Lure? The Seducer? The Other Woman?

Then what? She shuddered to think of it. There was the very real possibility that she could fall hopelessly in love with him. She was already very much under the spell of his magnetism.

She pushed all those unpleasant thoughts quickly from her mind without difficulty, since the flashing strobe lights and the thudding music were not conducive to rational planning.

Both the American and Dutch officers asked to see her again when they parted for the night, and she thanked them but politely explained that she was a recent widow and not dating. It darted through her mind that she had not entertained a single qualm about going out with Jacques, and she wondered if she was not using her widowhood as a convenient excuse. Jacques heard her refuse them and raised his eyebrows. It irked her that there was so little she could get away with in his presence.

Danielle kissed her Dutch officer good-bye. "*Au revoir*, Popeye, *mon petit chou*. Please to eat your *épinards*."

"That is spinach," corrected Jacques.

"That is spin—like to spin around?" She giggled and did a quick pirouette. "How I love the English. It is so visual a language. You see, I am spinning like the *épinards*!"

"I have never in my life seen spinach spin," commented Jacques as they started the car.

"That is because you know nothing about the *cuisine*.

Isn't that right, Simone? Ariane? In a *salade* of spinach, you must spin the spinach to make the oil and vinegar stick. If you cook it in a pot, you must spin it around your fork." There was no arguing with Danielle's analysis of language.

When they got to Simone's, Jacques walked her to the door and kissed her good night. "Let us see if it is a very passionate kiss," Danielle whispered to Ariane. Ariane did not want to look, but curiosity overwhelmed her. "Ah, pooh! It is not very passionate. Already it is finished," said Danielle. "He kisses her as if he were a Dutchman, in a hurry to get it over."

Ariane remembered the way Jacques had kissed her. It had been anything but hurried. Was he not as in love with Simone as everyone thought? And if they were lovers, why was he not spending the night?

She asked Danielle. "Who knows?" She gave a French shrug. "Simone's parents are at the moment on the Côte d'Azur. Perhaps it is because of her little boy."

As they entered the house, Danielle mumbled, "*Bonne nuit*. I danced so long I have no bottoms left on my shoes, and I am ready to drop. *À demain!*"

Jacques turned to Ariane. "I'm going down to the stable to check the horses. Do you want to come?"

She did want to check Willie's legs and apply another dose of ointment. The effectiveness of the treatment, she knew, depended on regular applications. But going down to the stable with Jacques at this time of night entailed its own complications. She turned the pros and cons over in her mind and, having decided that early morning would be soon enough to look at Willie's legs, she declined.

"Sleep on that job offer then, Ariane," he said softly, and before she knew what was happening, he had drawn her close. She felt his lips brush her cheek, her lips. As much as she wanted him to continue, she pulled away. Along with her jealousy of Simone crept in the same nagging suspicion that had plagued her marriage. Jacques needed her now just as Bud had—to help with the horses.

She had seen Bud often enough use people when he needed them, especially before a show. She had seen him turn on charm she had not even suspected he had. How much easier that would be for Jacques Valbonne with his indolent green eyes. It would be no great trick for him to bend a woman's will to his own, no matter what he wanted of her.

Horse training was founded on rewarding correct behavior, and he was renowned in the field. Did he think he could use the same methods on her, rewarding her work with the passion from his own body? What better way to make a woman docile and obedient to his whims?

Jacques stepped back, and in the dim light of the ancient hallway she saw the Valbonne ancestry etched into his sculptured face. He looked like a man who would use anything or anyone to get what he wanted. "Are you afraid that I only want you for what you can do with a horse—like you fear your husband did?"

She nodded. There was no use trying to lie to him.

"It would be impossible not to love a woman like you with great passion. Perhaps his mistake was not giving you enough physical proof of his love."

"Jacques!"

"No? You do not like to disturb the dust on a sacred memory? But even you talked about the trainers who can never bring a horse to capriole."

"And I suppose you have done it," she said dryly. She thought about the capriole, a complex maneuver in which the horse makes a giant leap in the air, the hind legs stretching out at the moment the horse's body is horizontal to the ground. The training requires such skill that it is hardly ever attempted.

She could see his white teeth in the darkness as he grinned at her. "Good night Ariane," he said as he strode out the door.

She stared after him, smiling bitterly to herself. If he were going to all this trouble to seduce her into working with his horses, he would surely be surprised to learn that the trainer he'd hired could not even sit in a saddle without collapsing from fear.

Chapter Six

ARIANE AWOKE EARLY the next morning to the sound of rain pounding on the window. She dressed quickly and went downstairs. An inviting loaf of fresh bread, butter, and jam were on the table so that she could prepare a *tartine* if she wanted one, and a maid magically appeared to ask if she would like coffee. "Not right now," she replied, despite the lure of breakfast. "I'm going to the stable."

"Just like Monsieur Jacques," said the maid, smiling. "He is always at the horses first, and then he thinks about his stomach." Ariane smiled at the woman's remark, then ran outside and over to the stable. She wished she had brought some high boots, as the rain was coming down quite hard now. She arrived out of breath.

"*Bonjour*," greeted Jacques. He was just coming out of Willie's stall.

"How is he?" she asked worriedly, though Jacques's expression had already told her that his condition was not very good. She slipped by him, and Willie nickered at her, happy to nuzzle against her. "Oh, my God!" she gasped. Three of his legs were down almost to normal, but the left hind leg that had given him so much trouble before was still badly swollen, worse than she had ever seen it. "Was he this way last night?"

"No. All the legs looked better."

"He must have knocked it against something during the night."

"That's what I was thinking. And I was hoping to let him exercise a little today, just walk him up and down,

72

but he can't seem to put any weight on that foot at all."

Ariane picked up Willie's hind leg gently, but he jerked it away from her. She looked up at Jacques, her brown eyes large with concern. "He never does this. The pain must be pretty bad." As if to confirm her assessment, Willie nudged her. "My poor Willie," she said, hugging him.

"Ariane," Jacques told her, his eyes locking onto hers, "I'm going to call the vet. He needs a shot of cortisone. That mixture of yours isn't strong enough to take care of that much swelling."

"Yes, it is," she countered firmly. "You just have to be patient and keep at it. It doesn't work overnight. You have to keep applying it at regular intervals. I should have come down here last night and done it." She felt miserably guilty now at having selfishly avoided Willie simply because she did not want to be alone with Jacques.

"Well, give it another try. But if there's no change by this afternoon, I'm calling the vet. There is no reason to let an animal suffer." His last words stung her like an accusation.

"Do you think I *want* to see him in pain?"

He ran a hand through his thick black hair. "No, of course not," he said more gently. "I know you have a lot of faith in those chemicals—but Willie is my horse now, and I'm going to have to treat him the way I think best. That must be understood."

She glanced sadly at Willie, feeling on the verge of tears. In her mind she knew that Willie was no longer her horse, but this was the first time she understood emotionally what that meant. No one had ever before dictated to her how to take care of him. Not even Bud. He had often made suggestions which she respected, but he had always gone along with her final judgment on any of the horses.

"I understand," she said weakly and went down to the tack room to get the ointment.

A few minutes later, as she was wrapping Willie's legs, she heard Jacques's voice behind her. "I've finished feed-

ing the horses, and I'm going up to the house to feed
myself. Come on up when you're through. We'll talk over
breakfast."

She nodded her assent without looking up at him and
kept on working. The ointment began to work immediately, and though the swelling would take a while to go
down, Willie was already putting some weight on the bad
leg. As his pain eased so did her conscience. She would
have to convince Jacques somehow that this was the best
way to go.

They were the only ones at the dining room table.
Jacques had spread a thick slice of bread with butter and
orange marmalade and was dipping the *tartine* into his
coffee from time to time. They sat silently for a few moments, then Ariane said, "He's already better, Jacques.
He even put some weight on the foot before I left."   .

"Good. I'm glad. It's stopped raining and the sun's
coming out. I'd like to see if he can walk a bit. It will be
good for the circulation."

"Let's let him fill his belly with hay first; it'll take him
a couple of hours. Then I'll walk him."

"You're not going to Paris today?" Jacques gave her
a sharp look.

"If you'd rather get rid of me so I won't bother you
about Willie, just say so. You're right. He's not my horse
anymore, and—"

"Ariane, I'd be glad to go along with your treatment,
but I am committed to an important horse show in a few
weeks. I've got ten horses to get ready and I have no help
now. To baby a lame horse and also worry about the others
is a lot of work."

"It's a big show?"

"The most important national exhibition of the year.
I have several horses that may qualify for the Olympics
entered in fifth level."

"But I could show Danielle how to take care of Willie.
She could do the wrapping. It's not that hard, and Willie
likes her."

"One cannot depend on Danielle." He sighed. "She may decide tomorrow to fly to Rome, to Majorca. Who knows? Ariane, I know you are hesitant to stay here. I understand, and I am not pressuring you. Believe that. But one day you are going to have to come to the realization that Wicked Willie is no longer your horse, that you cannot be there with a handkerchief every time he sneezes. But for the next few weeks I give you that option. You can even sauté carrots *au vin* for him for all I care, and I will pay you very well for helping me with the other horses. At night, I shall not as much as even attempt to steal a kiss from your beautiful lips, if that is what is bothering you."

She sipped her coffee without looking at him, then decided to tell him the whole problem. "I don't think you fully understand, Jacques." She looked up at him helplessly. "When I said I was through with horses, it wasn't just that I had decided to forget them. I can't *ride*, Jacques. That's the main problem. Ever since the accident, whenever I'm in a saddle, my knees go weak and my throat goes dry. It's fear washing over me—galloping, total unreasonable fear."

"But you're not afraid to work around horses. I've seen you with Willie. You went running out in the meadow at midnight without a shadow of fear crossing your face over what you knew was a dangerous expedition!"

"I guess I didn't stop to think about it then. I was half asleep when we started, drenched and numb by the time we reached him. But you saw me that morning on the ship's ramp, Jacques. I was petrified."

"I was frightened myself. Only an idiot wouldn't be. That was a dangerous situation. Anything could have happened."

"The difference between us is that you can still maintain your equilibrium and think when you're afraid. I can't. You could pay me a million dollars and I wouldn't be worth a cent to you."

"Riding horses, handling problem horses like Willie was that morning, is only a small part of getting horses ready for a show. You know that, Ariane. They must be groomed and clipped, worked on a longe line. I have two colts I'd like to put in a halter class. I can manage the actual riding if you take care of the rest and keep Willie doctored for me. That alone is going to take a lot of effort."

"I don't know." She shook her head. It all sounded logical enough. She knew there was a great deal she could accomplish for him, and it would give her more time to treat Willie.

"Let me try it for a day or two," she said finally. "If it seems to work out and we're both satisfied, then I'll stay the extra weeks."

"That's fine with me," he said brightly, "and it will give me time to make some calls. If you decide not to stay, I'll be able to find out which trainers are available and get some help."

She looked out the long French windows. Shafts of sunlight pierced the heavy clouds and cast golden shadows on the terrace, and she was reminded of their first drive together. "You were right about the clouds here, Jacques."

He smiled at her over his coffee. "You will learn to love Flanders."

She went upstairs to hang up her jacket now that the sun was out and was surprised to find her bed, which she had carefully made that morning, in complete disarray. Sheets, blankets, pillowcases were hanging over various chairs around the room. The window was opened wide, and a cool, fresh breeze made the sheets flap like sails on a clipper ship. Then she realized what had happened. A maid had evidently been there while she was at the stable and was airing everything out. It struck her as a delightful custom.

It was not only the sheets that were aired, she learned after she returned downstairs. As she reentered the dining room she saw that the French doors were opened wide and the maids were carrying heavy pieces of furniture out onto the terrace. "Do you do this every day?" she asked them.

"Once a week, *madame*. The furniture is many hundreds of years old, and the air here is very damp. If it does not go out, there is a not very pleasant odor. This way it is always like new."

Danielle made her way sleepily into the dining room with a yawn. Her blond curls stuck out in several places, and her blue eyes were puffy with sleep. "Ariane! You rise with the chickens! You and my brother make a good pair. Why anybody wants to see the sun come up is a mystery! For me, it is only when I do not go to bed the night before. That is natural. But to get up early is unnatural for human beings. You had a good time last night?"

Ariane nodded.

"But you didn't dance. How could you have a good time and not dance?"

"It's possible."

Danielle shook her curls in disbelief and reached for the butter to prepare a *tartine*. "I must show you some steps to do. Ah, but you leave today for Paris! *C'est dommage!*"

"No, Danielle, it's really not a shame, not yet." Danielle's curiosity was piqued.

"There's been a change of plans. I'm going to stay and help Jacques for a few days, maybe longer."

Danielle raised her eyebrows. "I think something went on last night after I went to bed, eh?"

"No, nothing like that." Ariane felt her face flush.

"No? But you turn very prettily pink!"

"Really, it's just to help out with the horses until he can find another trainer."

Danielle's face fell. "That I can believe. It is like my brother." She devoured another *tartine*. "While he should be seducing you with sweet murmurs of love and dozens of roses, he thinks only of his horses. *Dégoutant!* 'Disgusting' is the word?"

Ariane nodded. Perhaps it was.

Jacques was exercising one of his horses in a sheltered ring not far from the stable. Ariane stood quietly just inside the door to watch.

The horse moved out into the even-gaited canter while

Jacques, in complete control, seemed to do nothing. How deceptive a good rider is, thought Ariane. A nonequestrian would think that he was simply sitting there, letting the horse do all the work. It took years, she knew—hours and hours of arduous training—to be able to sit a horse like that controlling him all the while yet making the ride look effortless. And a horse had to be so sensitively trained that the slightest pressure of a leg muscle, the tiniest movement of a little finger would suffice to make him change gaits or direction.

Jacques slowed the horse into a trot, posting in exact rhythm with the horse's steps. Ariane noted that his legs did not move a fraction of an inch, for he posted correctly from the knees, using only the powerful muscles of his thighs to propel himself up and down in the saddle. Something inside her fluttered as she watched his well-muscled thighs, and though she tried to dismiss it, it only grew stronger as she recalled how close were the rhythmic movements to those of making love.

As though he read her thoughts, Jacques looked directly at her and smiled; then almost immediately he impelled the horse into a difficult piaffe in which the horse, instead of trotting ahead, lifted his legs high in place, springing into the air. There was a long moment of suspension between the time he rose up and the time he touched the ground. As with the training of a ballet dancer, it took years of patient, skillful work to teach a horse to execute such a difficult and beautiful movement. But Jacques compounded his feat by bringing the horse directly to passage—the same type of movement but one in which the horse moved forward.

The sight of Jacques and the horse together, as though they were floating on invisible wings around the ring, took Ariane's breath away. She had seen many performances of *haute école* riding before but none quite so beautifully done.

"What do you think?" he called to her.

"You're showing off." She laughed.

"Right. I'm trying to impress you."

"You are succeeding," she said with breathless admiration.

He brought the horse into a canter, and she held her breath, knowing instinctively what he was going to do next by the glint in his green eyes.

Suddenly the horse leaped high in the air, and just at the moment his body was parallel to the ground he kicked out his hind legs. It was an exquisite suspension. And Ariane shared with Jacques the exhilarating moment of triumph: the capriole.

Though she herself had never attempted it, she had loved jumping fences and knew the intense feeling of soaring into space, a powerful horse beneath her, and as she watched Jacques she felt that elation again, though it was tempered with regret. As much as she longed to be on the horse's back being propelled skyward, she knew those days were past. If she could not even bear to be in a saddle, how could she jump? How could she ever again aspire to a capriole?

Jacques dismounted and came over to her. "You deserve your reputation," she said to him while patting the nose of his horse. "That was exquisite work. The only thing I've ever seen that comes close was a performance I saw in New York of the Lipizaner Stallions."

"Where do you think I picked that up?"

"You attended the Spanish Riding School in Vienna?" she asked, surprise in her voice.

"Only for a year. I was learning a great deal, but the protocol was not to my taste. On entering the riding hall, you must salute the portrait of Emperor Charles VI—a man who died in the eighteenth century! Then there is saluting your instructor, saluting your horse—"

"Your horse?"

"I exaggerate only slightly, but the rules and regulations are, for a person not of Prussian military persuasion, impossible to obey. I obey only my own rules."

"And then feel free to break them," she added.

He smiled. "You already know me well, Ariane. Come, let's see how you work with a longe line."

Ariane showed him the methods she had used with the long rein to guide and direct a horse in training. With the exception of a few minor details, her techniques were the same as his.

"You have excellent hands," he complimented her. "I've always maintained that the touch should be light and elastic—for horses, anyway."

She ignored his innuendo and continued working with a two-year-old mare that was still being broken. Ariane was patient as the horse flew into a canter when only being asked to trot, and gently, gradually, she decreased the animal's speed.

"They trust you, Ariane. You can accomplish anything you want, for you have the patience and the skill." On hearing his words of praise, she suddenly wanted to show Jacques how she rode, too. She knew she was one of the best and had the blue ribbons and trophies to prove it. If only . . .

"I'd love to see you ride," he said, reading her thoughts.

Perhaps she would try again. Her whole life was different now, a new environment, new horses. It was not like being at the farm, where every nook and cranny reminded her of Bud, made her remember the terrible accident. Here, perhaps, things could be different.

As she worked the horses, she thought of the night before, the bored faces of the young people seeking to find stimulation in the artificial *caves* filled with electronic gimmickry. Had any one of them ever risen at dawn and cantered a horse across an open field? All the strobe lights in the world could not compare to the sensation of flying over a jump on the back of a horse.

By noon she was wishing she had eaten more *tartines*, as the main meal was not until two o'clock. She felt some irritation at Danielle for not even coming down to look at Wicked Willie's legs. Ariane began to wonder if she had been such a good judge of character back in New York when she had decided to sell Willie to her. It was fortunate that Jacques Valbonne was here to take on the responsibility. But he had so many good horses; Willie would never be special, as he was to her. Never again would he receive the love and affection she had lavished on him since he was a colt.

Then suddenly a new idea occurred to her. It was not a matter of money. The sale of the farm and horses had left her well off. Why not buy Willie back? Jacques would be well rid of the problem, and Danielle had certainly shown indifference. But where would she go with him? Back to the U.S.? He certainly couldn't travel with a bog spavin. Without room to move around on a ship, his condition would only get worse.

And even if she did keep Willie, what would she do with him? Find someone else to ride him because she was still afraid?

If he had to be somewhere, she concluded, the Valbonne stable was as nice a home as she could ever find. He would be well cared for, if not spoiled, exercised regularly, and shown in the finest exhibitions in Europe.

She checked Willie again, and the swelling had gone down further. She wrapped the legs again, then went back out to work the next horse. Jacques intercepted her. It was time for the midday meal. "You must be famished."

"I've barely gotten through half the horses you wanted me to work. It can't be two o'clock already!"

"You're more efficient than any trainer I've ever had. Bernard wouldn't even be through a fourth by now."

"At home I used to have it down to a routine, but I knew all my horses well, just where they needed the most attention. This is the finest group of horses I have ever seen, Jacques. I'm really impressed. I only wish I could ride them. The action on that black mare—she's as smooth as glass! I know if I worked with her in the ring I could make her transitions even better!"

Jacques's eyes lit up. "Would you like to try this afternoon? If you feel frightened, you can get off. But at least give it a try," he encouraged her.

"I'll see how I feel after lunch," she told him noncommittally. "I have the shakes now just thinking about it, but it may be because I'm hungry." The two walked back to the house.

Danielle gobbled her lunch quickly and, saying she had to be somewhere, left in a hurry. She was back in an instant. "Jacques, did you see where I left the newspaper?"

He didn't know, so she asked the maids, then scurried around for a few minutes until she found it. Tucking it into her purse, she flew out the door.

Jacques shrugged. "She must have found a special sale somewhere."

After lunch they walked back down to the stable. Jacques found a saddle that would fit Ariane and placed it on the black mare. The jitters Ariane had felt earlier had not abated and now increased as she watched Jacques fasten the cinch.

The mare was a gentle, good-natured horse. Ariane had handled her easily that morning on the longe line. It was the kind of horse she would have let her best students ride, training them both at the same time.

As they walked up to the enclosed ring beyond the stable Ariane patted the horse's neck and spoke affectionately to her, knowing this kind of contact was every bit as important as physical skill in riding. It was not an easy lesson to impress on children of the machine age, that horseback riding was not simply a matter of pushing the right buttons and shifting gears. A horse was an emotional creature with a need to be loved and appreciated. The greatest of horse trainers, Xenophon in 400 B.C., had urged trainers to use gentleness, understanding, and rewards. The Greek had told his disciples that a fearful horse would not perform well, and though not mean by nature, the animal could quickly turn vindictive without the correct handling. Bud's fatal mistake, in fact, had been to underestimate the malevolent fury of a new horse that had been badly mistreated by a former owner. But Bud's accident, at least the details of it, were still something Ariane could not bring herself to dwell on.

When they reached the ring, the mare's ears pricked up with interest. It was obvious she enjoyed working, and it was a tribute to Jacques that she did. "Here, I'll give you a leg up," he said, cupping his hands for her left foot.

She took a deep breath and swung her leg over. How familiar it felt to be in a saddle again. As a little girl, she had made saddles of everything: branches of trees, over-turned living room furniture, brick walls. From the age of two she had begged her father to take her to pony rides in the park, insisted on climbing up on a "real" horse at the age of three while they were vacationing in the Adirondacks. She had fond memories of the Saturday morning rental horses with their tough mouths and thick hides. They knew all the tricks for conveying timid children back to the stable.

How she had scoffed at her companions who broke down in torrents of tears when those ornery horses had refused to do as they wished. Her mounts always tried, but they never got away with a thing. She had been gutsy, even as a tiny child, kicking and yelling, bending those stubborn creatures to her will, cherishing every moment on their backs. How much she had had to "unlearn" when Bud had begun teaching her! But she had never lost her nerve—not until his death.

Mixed with the warming familiarity of the saddle was the trembling fear that gripped her chest, making it hard to breathe. Automatically she adjusted the stirrups, but her hands were shaking badly. The mare would be sensing all that, she knew. Perhaps it would be better to get off right away.

Jacques moved to the side, and Ariane closed her eyes for a moment, trying to bring her rapid breathing down to a steady rhythm, but her heart was pounding too fast. Mustn't think about Bud, she told herself, though she saw him clearly before her eyes, riding the stallion he'd just purchased.

"The horse is a little crazy," Bud had said. "Owner had him high on drugs, beat the hell out of him. It'll take us a while to bring him down to earth, but he's well worth it. Just look at him, Ariane."

The words came back to her clearly now, ringing in her

ears as though they had just been spoken. She could see
Bud smiling as the horse reared dangerously in the air.
But she had not been frightened at that moment. She had
seen Bud handle hundreds of situations just as difficult.
She had even seen him fly off, laugh, and pick himself
up and march back over to the horse. She herself had
tasted the bitter dust in her mouth many a time. It was
something that came with the work. It was what made it
exciting. You were always dealing with another being that
possessed an unpredictable mind of its own.

She shortened the reins until she made satisfactory contact with the mare's mouth, collecting the horse under her,
then squeezed gently with the calves of her legs. The mare
walked forward.

Even this slight, ordinary movement frightened Ariane,
and she felt a queasy dizziness as she gazed down at the
ground. "Don't look down," she could hear Bud's riding-
school voice yelling at her when she was thirteen. "Keep
your head up, your heels down, your knees in, your back
arched." She had echoed the words hundreds of times in
her classes.

She remembered the timid children with their frantic
faces as they gripped the pommel of the saddle. She could
always pick out the children who would be good riders on
the first day. They had a look of confidence about them,
a naturalness in sitting the saddle. Those who showed
inordinate fear would never make it, and she was careful
to tell their mothers that first day. "If they are frightened
at a walk, then they will be stiff and fall off at a trot. Not
everyone can ride a horse. It's nothing to be ashamed of.
Don't forget, it's a very dangerous sport. They have good
reason to be afraid. Why not give them tennis lessons
instead?" It was a speech she had learned from Bud and
memorized. They might have lost some lesson money, but
many a relieved parent came back to thank them later. It
was partly what their riding academy reputation had been
built on. People knew Bud and Ariane would not waste
time teaching children for whom riding was impossible.

Now, after all these years, would she, too, have to take up tennis?

Trot, she commanded herself. She could not walk the horse forever around the ring, though the trainer in her worked on bending the horse correctly to the circle, making sure the mare's hind legs followed directly behind the front. Jacques's calm deep voice broke into her thoughts. "Just walk her around a few times, Ariane. Don't try to trot or canter. The main thing for you today is to relax, get used to it again—though I'm glad you're getting her bent correctly."

She smiled to herself. So he had noticed. Why wouldn't he? A man who could train a horse to the capriole would certainly recognize what she was doing.

Relax. It was also something she used to tell the children. Never before had it been a problem to her. It was something Bud had never had to tell her. Being on a horse had been as natural as sitting in a rocking chair. But relaxing now was something to work at consciously.

Beginning with her neck and shoulders, she loosened each tense muscle, moving down her back to her hips and legs. Even her ankles, she noted, were stiff. And miraculously, as she loosened her muscles, the mare also moved out with more freedom. The rhythm of the even steps became calming, and Jacques's quiet, approving presence gave her courage.

"I feel better." She smiled down at Jacques, who was standing at the center of the ring. "I'm going to take her into a slow trot."

"Good for you. You'll do fine."

She made contact with the horse's mouth and squeezed with her calves. The mare hesitated at first, not sure of what was expected, but at the gentle, insistent urging soon broke into a jog trot. Just as she had suspected when she had put the horse on the longe line, her gait was as smooth as glass; she was no trouble to sit.

Ariane was feeling better, much more confident. She gave the aids again with her legs, collecting the horse

under her, and moved into a full trot. Out of the corner
of her eyes, she saw that Jacques had a wide grin.

"Already her transitions look better," he said with admiration. His encouragement was especially welcome to
her. The old cringing fear in her chest had almost completely disappeared as she put her mind to the training.

Feeling enough confidence now, she turned the horse
at a trot across the ring to change hands, and as she came
up on the wall she gave a slight pressure with her left leg.
The mare at first only trotted faster, but Ariane was per-
sistent and finally made the correct transition into a canter.
It was a pleasant, rocking gait which the mare assumed.
As Ariane followed the mare's head through the reins she
had a sense of well-being she had not known in months.

After cantering the mare around the ring once, she
decided to change hands again to make sure the correct
foreleg was leading. The horse, she discovered, had yet
to learn flying lead changes. Something else to work on.
It would not be difficult. Intelligent and limber, this mare
was eager to please.

Then suddenly Ariane noticed some movement outside
the door as she neared it. It was little Pierre running toward
them. Fear clutched her chest. Hadn't anyone told him
never to run up to where horses were being ridden? Thou-
sands of years of instinct made horses jump at any sudden
action or sign of pursuit. It was one of the reasons they
survived so well in the wild.

"Easy now," she said as calmly as she could while she
applied the reins, pulling back gently, still maintaining the
rhythm of the neck. To stop sharply would be to throw
the horse off balance, risk making her trip. But the running
child was bound to frighten the mare.

Bud flashed again across her mind. It had been a dog
running past the stable that day. The already edgy stallion
had become a maniac, rearing and kicking, bucking to
throw Bud off. Why hadn't he just slipped off? Why had
he insisted on staying on? The stallion had jerked around
and around, twisting and throwing his head back. It had

been the throwing back of the horse's head that had knocked Bud unconscious, making him finally drop off and slide under the powerful hooves. Another horse might have walked away, but the viciousness of that drug-crazed stallion had been insatiable. Before Ariane could get to Bud, before anyone could get to him, the animal had whirled around on his heel to pound Bud's chest, stomping with all his fierce, angry might.

Pierre was bounding up to the open door and the mare, seeing him for the first time, became frightened. Ariane's own tension did not help. The horse jumped quickly to the side. Ariane was drenched in panic. She felt herself flying up out of the saddle, losing her balance. But quick reflexes, born of years in just such situations, made her thighs tighten appropriately and bring the horse back under control. But she was shaking fiercely now. It was impossible to see anything before her eyes but Bud's body lying there lifeless in the dust. She brought the mare to a halt and dismounted limply, her shaking legs almost too weak to support her.

Jacques was furious at Pierre. "I've told you before never to run up here from the stable when horses are being worked. You know better than that!"

Pierre hung his head. "I forgot. I was just so anxious to come to the ring. I knew you had the black mare out, and I thought you might let me ride her."

"You're not going to ride any horse until you know how to act around them!" Jacques sternly reprimanded. "You can clean out stalls today. That's about all you're good for!"

Jacques slipped a protective arm around Ariane. "You all right?"

She nodded, catching her breath.

Pierre was humiliated, his eyes brimming with tears. "If she is supposed to be such a good trainer from the United States, how come she gets frightened just because a horse spooks?"

"It's none of your business," said Jacques harshly.

"Please, Jacques," Ariane begged him. "Pierre is right. I shouldn't be riding if I can't handle a minor situation like that. Let him ride the mare. Here, Pierre"—she turned over the reins—"I want to see you ride. Jacques has told me how good you are."

"It is all right?" Pierre asked Jacques timidly.

"Yes, go ahead. But you must use your head around horses. That was a very stupid thing you did."

Pierre shot an undisguised look of hatred at Ariane—as though she were directly responsible for the reprimand he received from Jacques—which unnerved her. Was Pierre so indoctrinated by his mother that he too could not bear the thought of Jacques with another woman?

As Pierre moved the horse out, Ariane was once again struck by how much he resembled Jacques, even to the way he sat a saddle. He could indeed have been a miniature of Jacques. Did Pierre know the truth about his father? Was that why he was so anxious to protect his mother's interests?

The boy's riding took her mind off these thoughts. He handled the horse very well for a child his age. He had a natural balance, an instinct for what to do that could not be drummed into the smartest of children. They either had equestrian ability or they did not.

She could see that Jacques took immense pride in Pierre, and even though he corrected the child, he was proud of his horsemanship. Watching Pierre handle the mare made Ariane angry at herself. If a ten-year-old boy could ride the horse with such calm assurance, why couldn't she—an experienced twenty-seven-year-old woman? Pierre might have been brutal with his comments, but he was right.

Ariane turned to leave the ring. "I've got to work the other horses," she told Jacques.

"Tomorrow you must ride again," he said as he looked at her steadily.

"Maybe," she replied noncommittally.

* * *

When Simone arrived that afternoon to pick up Pierre, Ariane was surprised to hear Jacques say that he was too busy to chat with her.

"You will be over tonight?" Simone pressed him. "I am preparing *boeuf Bourguignon*. I know how you like that, *mon cher*."

"Not tonight," he said abruptly.

Simone was not one to let something slide past. "Why not?"

"I've made other plans."

Simone's eyes widened, and she glared openly at Ariane. "Oh, very well, I see."

Jacques let her get huffily into her sparkling white Mercedes without offering further explanation. Even Ariane was shocked at his sudden coldness and, seeing Pierre's distress, she felt impelled to smooth over the rebuke to his mother. She still felt guilty about Pierre's having been scolded for her poor handling of the mare. Now he probably blamed himself for the way Jacques was treating his mother.

"It was a pleasure to watch you ride today," she said to Pierre, as he got into the car. "I've taught a lot of kids in my time, and you are one of the best I've ever seen."

Pierre puffed up with pride at her compliment. "Today I rode a horse," he told his mother, "that *she* could not even ride, and she is supposed to be a real trainer."

Ariane smiled wanly to herself. So much for good intentions.

"Pierre," sighed Simone, "you must not tell fibs."

"He's right," said Ariane weakly. "He rode much better than I did."

"Odd that Jacques should keep on an incompetent as a trainer," she mumbled loud enough for Pierre to hear but not loud enough for Jacques. "Or maybe not so odd," she added, glaring at Ariane. "You must have other talents he can use."

Before Ariane could express her indignation, Pierre said, "Tomorrow Jacques is going to let me practice jumping the mare over the two-foot fence."

Simone now focused her fury on Jacques and said, this time loud enough for him to hear, "Tomorrow Pierre has other plans." Ariane noted that she was precise in repeating Jacques's exact excuse to her.

"What other plans?" Jacques came over to the car, a menacing expression in the depths of his green eyes.

"Maman!" cried Pierre.

"Pierre, you cannot be over here bothering Jacques every day when he is working so hard with his new trainer to get horses ready for a show," she said sarcastically.

It was clear that Simone was ruthlessly using her child as a weapon to strike back at Jacques, and Ariane could see that she had cleverly hit her mark.

"Pierre is no trouble," said Jacques quickly. "In fact, he is a big help to me and Ariane."

"Please, Maman, can't I come over tomorrow?" Pierre's voice was laden with desperation. Ariane ached for him, and she knew Jacques did, too.

"We'll see," Simone said coldly, addressing her words directly to Jacques as she turned the ignition key.

Ariane returned to work silently, blanketing the horses for the night, giving them their grain. She was dying to ask Jacques about the scene that had just transpired between him and Simone, but she didn't dare. His mood seemed too black; she was afraid he would lash out at her.

Finally, as they walked up to the house, she took a deep breath and said, "Was it worth all that not to be with Simone tonight?"

Jacques slipped an arm around her shoulders, and she felt the pleasant warmth of him infuse her.

"Yes, because tonight I am going to make you a Belgian omelette and then we are going to take a tour of Bruges canals by night."

She remembered the picturesque little boats floating along the illuminated canals from the night she had had dinner with his father.

"Are you sure you want to do that? It sounds a little like candlelight and romance—not at all your style."

"You would be surprised to find out what is my style." He took her head in the crook of his elbow playfully and tousled her long auburn hair. She had seen him do much the same thing to a three-month-old filly earlier that afternoon.

"Why do you laugh?" he said, grinning at her.

"I think you treat your women like you do horses."

"No, there you are wrong. I have always given much better treatment to my horses."

She thought of the cold way he had just treated Simone and had to agree.

Chapter Seven

WHEN THEY GOT back to the house Danielle greeted them. She seemed depressed, but anything less than her usual exuberance could be categorized under the heading of depression, thought Ariane.

"Vladimir called. He's here from Paris on his yearly pilgrimage."

Jacques laughed. "But I thought you were madly in love with Vladimir. Or was that last year?"

"That was last year. Don't you remember he was going to jump off the Eiffel Tower if I didn't marry him?"

"If he's still around and you're still not married, that's a pretty good indication that he's reconsidered," noted Jacques.

"He is always going to do something rash as a result of something else," moaned Danielle. "We were at a Russian restaurant once and he didn't like the Chicken Kiev. He marched into the kitchen and punched the poor chef in the nose! I really shouldn't have said I'd see him, but he sounded so desperate this time."

"Vladimir always sounds desperate. I think it is his unstable noble Russian blood. You would do better to stick with the cool Dutchmen."

She sighed. "Dear Popeye. One could not find two men more extremely opposite than Christiaan and Vladimir. Poor Vladimir had too much instability in his early life," she explained to Ariane. "He is the grandson of a first cousin of the czar. He's been raised with a terror of revolutions and revolutionaries. If you even mention the word Bolshevik he flies into a rage."

"Is that such a hard word to avoid?" asked Jacques with amusement.

"You have no understanding of my problems, Jacques. Horses never worry about revolutions or Chicken Kiev or threaten to leap off the Eiffel Tower. Are you going to Simone's tonight?"

"No. Since it's the cook's night off, I am making an omelette for Ariane and taking her on a boat ride along the canals."

Danielle's spirits immediately perked up, and she clapped her hands together happily. "Wonderful! Vladimir and I will join you. I'll have him bring his balalaika and sing 'Ochy Chornia.' You will be absolutely ravished. I swear it. But his 'Kalinka,' with that tenor! The trouble is, he should have studied opera. I don't know why he insists on being a poet. He fancies himself a dashing Lord Byron, but it's so impractical in this day and age."

"It was impractical in Lord Byron's day, too," observed Jacques, and, intent on avoiding another evening with company he did not wish to keep, he said, "Dany, my dear, Ariane and I will take one boat and you and Vladimir and his balalaika can go dancing in Knokke."

"Jacques has no sense of the romantic," Danielle said with a sigh as she turned to Ariane. "Well, if you don't want us along, we shall go to the Scotch Club in Knokke."

As Ariane was thinking that she would prefer to have Danielle and her mad Russian poet along for protection, the doorbell rang. A maid ushered in the most melancholy man Ariane had ever seen.

Vladimir had limpid black eyes and brown hair falling across his forehead. He was tall and extremely handsome in an undernourished, poetic way, but he was shabbily dressed in faded, torn jeans. The balalaika was strapped to his back. She could see how a girl could be taken with him as he kissed Danielle's hand gallantly and presented her with a bouquet of lilacs. He was truly a man of the nineteenth century.

"He was not this bad until he saw *Doctor Zhivago* a few years ago," whispered Jacques. "It completely transformed him."

"He does look a little like Omar Sharif," she admitted.

"Say that to him and I shall never forgive you as long as I live," he whispered.

"Dmitry, this is our friend Ariane, who is visiting from New York," Danielle said as she brought him into the living room.

"Dmitry? I thought your name was Vladimir," she said, shaking his hand.

"Vladimir was Papa's idea," explained Danielle. "He thinks a Russian poet should be named Vladimir."

"Come now, Dany," added Jacques. "Our father thinks all Russians are named Vladimir."

"So many of them are," said Dmitry darkly. "One of Czar Nicholas's uncles was Grand Duke Vladimir. He was a close friend of my grandfather's. That is, before the unfortunate revolution that has devastated my country—"

"Dmitry, darling," interrupted Danielle, "let's go to the Scotch Club. It's so decadently capitalistic. Just what will amuse you."

"But I have come to Bruges to commune with the fifteenth century. I spent all day among the paintings of Van Eyck and Memling. You can't drop me back into the twentieth century. Why don't we take a boat ride along the canals? I have my balalaika and—"

"We can't do that, Vladimir."

"We *must*. There is nothing like lying flat on your back and gazing up at the brick buildings of Bruges while floating endlessly down the canals at night."

Danielle gazed helplessly at Jacques.

"Separate boats?" she suggested.

"Whatever for?!" protested Dmitry.

"Jacques wants to be alone with Ariane," said Danielle finally. "He's been after her since they met, and this is the first night he's managed to be alone with her."

Ariane tried not to blush, but her embarrassment made it impossible not to.

"Then we must protect her," said Dmitry gallantly, stepping between her and Jacques. "I will not stand by and see this poor girl seduced by Jacques Valbonne. Do you remember last year when you were both in Paris and I fixed him up with my third cousin Anastasia? She fell passionately in love with him, worshiped him like an icon. And he cast her aside cruelly. She was ready to leap off the Eiffel Tower with me."

"Dmitry, I only went out with her a few times!" protested Jacques.

"It was enough times for her to lose the flower of her innocence."

"Anastasia was about as innocent as—"

"Please!" said Danielle loudly.

"He is a man who loves only horses," Dmitry continued. "What kind of a man devotes his whole life to horses and casts aside a woman who loves him?"

"This from a man who writes one terrible poem a month and calls himself a poet?"

"That was cruel, Jacques," said Danielle.

"He *is* a cruel man," agreed Dmitry. "I don't wish to be with him at all tonight. Let us go to the North Sea and contemplate Neptune's infinite grandeur, the rising world of waters dark and deep...."

Danielle was pulling him out the door, so Ariane did not get a chance to hear the finale.

"Where does Danielle find these people?" Jacques said, shaking his head in wonderment.

Ariane had another question on her mind. "Did you really compromise Anastasia's innocence?"

Jacques laughed. "Anastasia's famed innocence, if she is to be believed, was compromised at the age of seventeen by Dmitry."

Ariane was amused by the poet's convenient forgetting of his own impropriety. Still, she had the fresh memory of how Jacques had behaved toward Simone. Was Anastasia but another casualty?

She considered the matter later as she took a luxurious hot bath in the huge European-style tub. Muscles she had forgotten about now ached, but it felt good to be physically active again. If her life was not to be spent around horses, she knew that she would eventually have to fill it with some form of vigorous outdoor exercise. As she massaged her arms and legs and leaned back in the hot water to soothe her neck, she thought back over the events of the day. Tomorrow, she vowed, she would ride that black mare, no matter what. No ten-year-old child was going to make her look like a fool!

Jacques was already in the kitchen when she came downstairs. It was the first time since she had been at the Valbonne estate that she had ventured into the kitchen. It looked like a painting by a Dutch artist with its black and white checkerboard tiled floor and tall, leaded glass windows. A huge room with a large table in the center, it was a kitchen designed to harbor many servants, certainly not one designed for a single harried housewife. There seemed to be no concession to modern conveniences: no garbage disposal, no dishwasher. Even the refrigerator was small. "I can't imagine being able to keep more than one meal at a time in there," commented Ariane.

"There's no need to; the maids shop every day. It is not like in the States with the supermarkets. In Bruges you must buy your meat at one place, the cheese at another, and the bread and eggs are delivered to us every morning fresh." He was already removing a basket of large eggs from the refrigerator.

"What can I do to help?"

He handed her some onions to chop and tomatoes to slice while he separated the egg whites from the yolks.

"I think you are baking a pie and not an omelette," she teased.

"No, you must wait and see how I do this. It is really

not Belgian at all, but my own invention."

His sleeves were rolled up, and Ariane was delighted to watch him deftly crack open the eggs, then whisk the whites until they were fluffy. He sautéed the tomatoes and onions together with a variety of spices. "This is really the secret to good cooking," he confided. "Spices."

"Just think, Jacques, if you ever want to give up horses, you can always get a job as a chef."

"You have not tasted anything quite so divine as my bouillabaisse." He kissed the tips of his fingers. "But this will give you a fine introduction to my culinary expertise. Now, don't stand there idle—you must grate the cheese. Do you enjoy cooking?"

"I love to fool around like this," she admitted. "Experiment with different things. Following a recipe, though, is a bore—so cut and dried. It's always more fun to be original, even if you create an inedible horror now and then."

"I agree with you. I have made some disastrous things, but I've never considered that a tragedy. A true cook must have courage." He folded the whites into the yolks with a finesse she would not have imagined of him, sprinkled the top with cheese, and after letting it heat on the stove for a while, put the whole mixture into the oven.

"Out of this world!" she exclaimed after her first bite.

"There are variations I must show you. I do one with mushrooms sautéed in wine."

"Mushrooms in wine—I love it already!"

Ariane was glad they were having dinner on the kitchen table, just the two of them without the hovering servants.

"This is really an old-fashioned Flemish kitchen," he told her. "Do you like it?"

"I like the size, the floor, and the windows, but it lacks warmth. Don't be insulted, Jacques, but it's really a rather dismal place."

He glanced around as though looking at it for the first time. "And if this were *your* kitchen, how would you decorate it?"

"Oh, maybe some flowered wallpaper there, white shutters, some hanging plants. I'd paint it a bright, cheerful color, maybe yellow, get a tablecloth to match. If I lived here I'd probably wind up eating all my meals in the kitchen rather than the formal dining room."

"And where would you have the maids eat? In the dining room?"

She laughed. "You have a point."

"What would you change about the dining room?"

She considered it a moment. "Nothing."

"You would redecorate the entire kitchen and do nothing about the dining room?"

"No. Definitely not. It has a personality all its own—like Bruges. If one comes to live here, one should expect to leave everything the way it is, the way it has been for centuries."

"You don't feel overwhelmed by the Valbonne ancestral ghosts?" he said with a wry smile, his green eyes twinkling.

She laughed. "Oh, yes! But it's a good warm feeling to live in a house that has seen so much, the continuity of the same family going on and on under the same roof. It's something most Americans, with their transitory way of life, never experience. It gives a person roots, a tradition. I would think that for children especially it would be wonderfully reassuring."

"It is," he said softly, with the same tone he had used that afternoon at Gruuthuse. "The bed where my father sleeps is where my mother gave birth to me and Danielle. It is in the same bed that my father was born—and his father before him. Those people are all around me here, and I feel very close to them." He reached over and took her hand.

In that moment she felt a link with all the Valbonne ancestors and longed to be a part of them through Jacques. He brought her hand to his lips and kissed her fingertips lightly without taking his eyes from her. It was the kind of chivalrous gesture that would have gone better with candlelight, but it was nonetheless breathtaking for Ariane even over a kitchen table.

"So you like my omelettes?" he said, jarring the mood.

"It is the most splendid omelette I have ever tasted. What is the French proverb about them? My mother used to tell me, but I have forgotten."

"In order to make an omelette, one must break some eggs."

She thought of Simone. In order to have Jacques, she would have to break that woman's hold on him. "And what does your friend Simone think of your omelettes?"

"What made you think of Simone?"

"I was thinking of her *boeuf Bourguignon* and *côtes de porc*. She must be quite a connoisseur of *haute cuisine*."

"She has never tasted one of my omelettes."

"Why not? Doesn't she trust your cooking?"

"I have never invited her into my kitchen."

"Then I have been honored with a rare privilege."

He was smiling as he ran the back of his fingers across her smooth cheek. "I've never invited any woman into my kitchen before, Ariane."

No confession of love over a candlelit supper with champagne could have had as devastating an effect as his last statement. It was as though he had allowed her into the inner sanctum of his soul, but her practical nature quickly stepped in and swept the idea away. Was it really a compliment to be invited into a man's kitchen? Simone would probably not put up with it, thinking she was being treated like a maid.

"You are also the only one who knows about Gruuthuse, Ariane." This new confession dispelled her suspicions. Another man might bestow precious gifts of jewelry on a woman; Jacques was a man who gave gifts of himself. Words were not necessary. She reached for his hand, and the understanding flowed through it into hers.

But it was only a brief moment before he stood to clear the plates. "You'd better dress in blue jeans and put on a heavy jacket. It can be freezing on the canals at night."

Then with a mischievous glint in his green eyes he added, "It's not nearly as romantic as you imagine."

"What does the weather have to do with romance?" she asked.

"It is impossible, I've found, to get very romantic when you are trying to maneuver your way through layers of clothing," he responded practically.

"Didn't anyone ever explain to you, Jacques Valbonne, that romance is not necessarily stripping naked?"

"No, but perhaps you can explain it to me later tonight. It is something that has puzzled me all my life."

Ariane liked the way the colored lights danced on the water, reflecting and spilling off the sculptured stone buildings. Gruuthuse was especially pretty by night, with its intricate lacework of stones and churchlike flying buttresses. They passed by several tourist boats in which guides were spouting out a plethora of information in French and English. "I'm glad you're not boring me with a lot of numbers tonight," she confided to Jacques. "Who cares if such and such was founded in the twelfth century and additions were made in the fourteenth century."

"My father would argue with you. He finds numbers fascinating."

"But if you fog up your mind with dates and events, you will miss the real beauty of these places."

"We think alike."

"But I would disagree with you about the romance here. It's wonderfully romantic floating along under the stars."

He navigated the boat over to the side of the canal and in the shadows of some overhanging branches. "Shall I take that as an invitation?"

"I was only *commenting*, not *inviting*," she said flatly.

"Good for you." He laughed and started the boat up again. "Making love in one of these small boats in very uncomfortable."

"You've done it?"

"I did many crazy things in my youth."

"With Simone?" The darkness provided her a cover of flippancy that she acutally did not possess.

Without giving her a direct answer he said, "When you are young, it is not always easy to find a place where you won't be discovered."

"Is it true that Pierre is actually your son?"

"That was direct!"

"Throw me overboard and make me swim home, but *never* accuse me of subtlety."

"It's one of the things I adore about you, Ariane. You are like a horse that way. Your emotions are all on the surface; nothing is hidden."

"I suppose, coming from you, being called a horse is a compliment, but you have evaded my question entirely."

"You wonder if Pierre is my son?"

"Forget I mentioned it, Jacques. It's none of my business." Suddenly, she didn't care to hear his response.

"I don't know if Pierre is or isn't," he answered her. "Does it matter to you?"

She tried her flippant voice, knowing full well he wouldn't be fooled for a moment. "Why should it matter to me?"

"Because it matters to me."

"Has Pierre been told that you are?" she asked quietly.

"No, of that I'm sure. And it is fortunate. The child has enough problems without having to worry about who his father is," he said bitterly.

"Then his fondness for you is because of the person you are, Jacques. It is the purest kind of love, based on esteem and admiration."

Jacques laughed. "Such high ideals! You talk like a *précieuse* from the seventeenth century."

"Esteem is not important to you?"

"Of course it is. I don't believe you can truly love someone unless you respect them. Passion dies very quickly, but if love is going to endure, much more is necessary."

She did not answer him, for his thoughts were arousing her own turbulent feelings.

Jacques broke the silence.

"You might as well go ahead and get all the questions out of your system. There is nothing worse than having unanswered questions between two people who are making love."

"What makes you so sure we are going to make love?"

"I know because I can see it in your eyes every time you look at me. You thought of little else while you watched me ride this morning. There is nothing more seductive than watching someone ride a horse, especially if there is an attraction."

"And that's what you were thinking when you watched me make a fool of myself on the black mare?"

"You handled that mare beautifully when she spooked. You tightened your leg muscles and held fast. A woman with strong limbs like that is wonderful in bed."

The low seductive tone of his voice made her heart pound. It was impossible to think of anything but tightening her legs around him as he spoke. She longed to make a statement of righteous indignation, but it would not have rung true. She had already learned how fruitless it was to lie to him.

As they rounded a corner, they heard the sound of beautiful music. "Oh my God," said Jacques, wheeling the boat around and back into the shadows.

"What's the matter?"

"Can't you hear it?"

"Yes, it sounds lovely—what is that, a guitar?"

"No, a balalaika, for God's sake!"

"Vladimir and Danielle must have decided to come here after all."

Jacques found a small private dock under one of the houses and pulled the boat up, slipping the rope around. "Here, lie down and they'll never see us."

She scooted down, and Jacques quickly stretched out next to her. He had been right. It was not a very comfortable place for making love, but as he slipped his strong arms around her, she felt it might be possible to forget the discomfort.

The balalaika music grew louder. "At least he's not singing," whispered Jacques. "Are you cramped for space?"

"No, I'm fine."

She rested her head on his shoulder and looked up at the stars. He turned her face to him, then kissed her lightly on the lips, his free hand caressing her cheek.

As their kisses grew more intense, he unzipped her heavy jacket and slid his hand inside, pushing up her sweater. For a brief second she felt her nipple harden, uncovered in the icy cold of the night, and, just as quickly, it was covered again by the searing heat of Jacques's hard tongue flicking across the tip, sending flames of desire pulsing through her body. How like a horseman, she thought wildly, to be able to take the slightest of movements and use it for shattering impact.

The balalaika music with its haunting tremors echoed across the winding Bruges canals and into her soul. She gasped as Jacques slid an exploring hand down across the soft vulnerable skin of her belly. She wanted him now with a screaming fury of desire. The equestrian did not waste his power, knowing exactly where his skillful touch would bring the maximum response, and she eagerly obeyed his commands, wanting to please him, giving more of herself with each sigh.

Suddenly a window opened just above them. They froze. An angry voice yelled across the canal. "You there with the rotten music! Don't you have any respect for people trying to sleep?"

"A curse upon the next five generations of your descendants, *monsieur*!" shouted Dmitry.

Several more windows opened.

"Cut out the racket!"

"It's late!"

"Can't a person get any sleep!"

"Blasted tourists! There ought to be a city ordinance against these boats at night!"

"Dear citizens of Bruges," they heard Dmitry say as they saw him stand up precariously in the small boat, gesturing dramatically with his balalaika. "I bring you music from the agonized depths of my Russian soul, and yet you shun me!"

"Go back to Russia, you crazy Bolshevik, and leave us in peace!"

"Bolshevik?!" The small boat began to rock, and they heard Danielle say worriedly, "Vladimir, sit down, we're going to tip over."

"You're a nation of small-minded shopkeepers!" Dmitry hurled at them. "May the Bolsheviks march through your hardened bourgeois hearts and hang red flags from your belfry!"

Ariane and Jacques tried to stifle their laughter for fear of being discovered.

"Come on, Vladimir," pleaded Danielle. "Oh, I knew we should have gone to the Scotch Club."

The magic spell had been more than broken by the ruckus. Jacques waited until all the windows were safely shuttered again and angled the boat back out into the canal. "We'll circle around a bit until Vladimir is back in. There is no sense running the risk of him finding us. When he starts on one of those tirades, he goes on for hours."

There were lights on in the house as they drove up, and the strong voice of a tenor accompanied by a balalaika wafted its way down the drive. As they got out of the car, they heard Danielle joining Dmitry on the chorus.

> *"Ka-lin, a ka-ka-lin, a ka-ka-lin,*
> *A-ka-ka lin, kam-ay-a."*

"'Kalinka,'" muttered Jacques. "The two of them get going with that and we'll never hear the end of it. Danielle's crazy about Russian music. Once named a poor little dog of ours 'Kalinka.'"

"I'd like to check Willie out, wrap his legs again as long as we're back here," she suggested.

They walked down to the stable, and Jacques helped

her with the wraps. Wicked Willie yawned with indifference as they worked, and Ariane found herself yawning back in self-defense.

"Are you tired?"

"No, it's just that Willie and I get started like this and it's hard to stop. I told somebody once about having a yawning marathon with my horse and they thought I'd gone mad." She laughed. "Why is it that people never attribute any personality to horses? I've seen women talk baby talk to their toy poodles and look at me as though *I* were nuts when I claimed to have an intelligent chat with Willie. Right, Will?"

Willie nudged her sleepily, then leaned his head against her chest and closed his eyes.

"You should not have sold this horse," said Jacques. "Never in your life will there be another as dear to you, Ariane."

"I worry more about him than about myself, I think."

"Oh, he'll get along all right. Horses become attached to other horses. They can do very well without us as long as they have companions."

She rested her own head against Willie's and patted his silky neck. "Everyday I wonder if I did the right thing. But if you had seen me a month ago—I had no other choice. How quickly a person's life can change around. Like the ripples you talked about. One stone in the water and it goes on and on."

As they checked the other horses, the black mare stuck her head out of the stall and nickered at Ariane. "*À demain, ma vieille*," she said laughingly. "Tomorrow, we'll see what you and I can do."

Jacques smiled. "You're going to do well tomorrow."

"I'm glad you have confidence."

"Ariane, you hardly know your own potential for riding—or for making love."

They headed back up to the house, where the tenor voice assaulted them again from an open window. "*O-chy chor-ni-a, O-chy ias-ni-a.*"

"Do you really want to hear that?" he asked her.

"Do we have any choice? I mean it's not like a stereo you can turn off by pressing a button."

"I know where we can go." He took her hand and led her back toward the stable, but instead of going in they went around to the side.

Crossing a patio, Jacques lifted up a pot of tulips and, producing a key, opened a heavy door. There was a narrow hallway, then Ariane heard a clinking sound. It was dark, but she could see Jacques was holding back what looked like a beaded curtain for her to pass through.

He lit one candle, then another. "There are no electrical outlets here. It used to be a stable master's house, but Dany and I with all the energy of teenagers transformed it one summer."

Jacques started a glowing fire in the ancient brick fireplace, which bathed the room momentarily in light.

"Talk about being transported into another era!" she said, amazed. "For Bruges it is the fifteenth century, but here in this room one is back in the sixties! A Beatles poster, a 'Make Love Not War' sign." She took a closer look at the beaded curtain and found to her surprise that it was made solely of bottle caps pressed around string. "How long did it take you to make this?"

"Practically the whole summer." He laughed. "We had all our friends collect bottle caps, then we'd come back here and drink beer and make those things."

It was a cozy room, painted brick-red, with overstuffed, comfortable furniture. In the corner was half of a wagon that had been made into a bar. "We found this in back of the stable and decided that with the wheel it would make a perfect bar. Would you like a glass of cognac?"

"Good idea."

"I have the maid come out here at least once a week to keep the room from getting too dusty. I don't use it much anymore, but it's a nice place to get away when you need it—like tonight. Sometimes I just come in here from the stable instead of walking back up to the house. In the summer we have some chairs out on the patio, and it is very pleasant to have tea in the afternoon."

He brought the snifters of cognac over and settled in next to her on the couch. "Well, how do you like my little hideaway?"

"I like it." She smiled and put her feet up on the scarred, handmade wooden coffee table. "Not everywhere do you feel privileged to put your feet on somebody's coffee table."

"Kick your shoes off if you like." He unlaced his own and shed his heavy jacket. The crackling fire was already making the small room quite warm, so she did the same.

They fell silent for a moment, staring at the fire, each knowing exactly what the other was thinking. What was there to stop them now from completing what had begun earlier in the boat?

She felt a tingling sensation wash over her as she remembered the way he had lifted her sweater, exposing her naked breast to the icy night air, then covered it with the searing heat of his mouth, his hard tongue dancing across her nipple.

She remembered watching him ride that afternoon, and as she looked down out of the corner of her eye she remembered the thrill of seeing his long, hard-muscled thighs gripping the stallion's back as he moved in rhythm with the graceful passage.

Jacques reached for her hand and kissed her fingertips as he had done earlier in the kitchen, but he continued staring into the fire. "I want you, Ariane," he said quietly, though he made no move toward her.

She stifled the overpowering urge to throw her arms wildly around his neck. "I . . . I want you, too, Jacques. Part of me does, anyway. And part of me will fight against it." She clasped his hand tightly, trying to release some of the tension that was building up inside her.

"Why should you fight it?" He forced her to look into his dark green eyes, which reflected the flames. His skin had taken on the golden-red hues of the fire, though part of his face was hidden in the shadows. His was a face as beautifully sculptured as the Gruuthuse which he loved.

She drew a finger along the line of his dark straight eyebrow, across the high cheekbone, then down onto his full, sensuous lips, which looked scarlet in the warm light and were curved into a smile.

"Let me tell you all the things you fear, *chère* Ariane, for in the few days I have known you, I have studied you. You are a passionate and sensitive woman. All your life you have poured this love into your work. And ours is not a profession that pays you back in gold. No, many of us die in the poorhouse. We stay with the horses because, for every gesture of kindness we show them, they return it a hundredfold. They perform for us; they give us the ultimate of experiences—fly us through the air, propel us like thunder across vast expanses of space, and turn us into ancient centaurs, rulers of the universe. And when we bring them back to earth, they nuzzle us and wipe away our tears, share our every joy. And so in need of love are we that we devour it gladly, gratefully. Our wives and husbands and lovers are not nearly as unselfish, and so much more demanding of us that we eventually turn them away. We think we will never have human love as intense and all-encompassing as the love of our powerful four-footed friends. So we give up. We settle for less in our human relationships.

"And now sitting here with me, Ariane, for the first time in your life, you suspect that life may have more to offer you. That there may be a thrill as intense as a full gallop across a meadow at dawn. And you're afraid of that. For it goes against everything you've led yourself to believe all your life."

She gazed into the fire and felt a deep longing to shed tears. What he said was true, all of it, and the pressure of his hand on hers told her that he knew because he felt the same.

"You rode again today, Ariane. Do you have the courage to learn what our love can be?" He pushed away her long auburn hair and caressed her neck, letting his large hand slide meaningfully across her breast. She shuddered with growing passion.

"Can you take the capriole?" he whispered as his mouth came down on hers.

Instinctively he had found the weakest link in her argument against involvement. The competitive rider in her that always pushed her far beyond her capabilities reached out for him. She slid her hands under his thick woolen sweater and explored his chest, finding his own silken nipples and making them grow hard under her touch.

She moved her lips softly against his, running her tongue across them to better taste their sweetness, knowing how the rest of his body would taste when they were naked and damp with love.

He was forcing her with his weight down on the couch and she acquiesced willingly, pulling him onto her, exploring the taut horseman's muscles of his powerful back. She wanted to be tight against him, at one with him. He was pushing her sweater up as he had done on the boat, but this time he slid it up quickly over her head, leaving the top half of her body exposed. "You are beautiful, Ariane, my beautiful silken Ariane." She smiled up at him, arching like a cat as he made long sweeping caresses with his strong hands, first of her bare white shoulders, then of her breasts, taking the burgundy nipples between his white teeth, twisting them into exquisite frenzy as his hands swept over her ribs and pressed into her lower belly.

Never stop, she thought frantically to herself. Never stop loving me like this, Jacques.

His hands were molding her to him with their powerful, knowing strength. She was helpless now. There was nothing that could keep her from giving him all her love. He had tamed her as surely as he tamed a wild filly. She would gladly do anything for him, be anything he wanted. He deftly pulled the last vestiges of her covering away, his lips moving steadily, kissing, probing, tasting across the soft skin below her breasts. His hands pushed her legs apart, squeezing her thighs as she resisted him. Her screaming passion doubled. She was like a madwoman dispossessed of her own body, which made its own raging demands now, rising and falling and retreating to the subtle fiery movements of the equestrian.

She was crying and laughing, letting him guide her. He held the reins, but she had the ultimate power to excite, changing the rhythm of her gait, now smooth, now full of frenzy at a full gallop, bringing him to the cliff's edge, then wheeling around to race across an open meadow, her flaming red mane flying into his face in the icy hot wind.

She lay peacefully across his warm damp body. He was still caressing her, and as he touched certain places the embers of her passion stirred, then faded again. She nuzzled his strong neck, and he kissed her forehead.

"Was it what you expected, Ariane?"

"No, Jacques." Her mouth was dry and she found it hard to form words. "Look at me, I am still shuddering under your touch. It was like riding, like you described, only more so—a thousand capriole leaps in the air. I never would have thought it was possible, not in a million years. Don't ever leave me, Jacques! Now that I know this, I could never live without you."

He remained strangely silent.

"Jacques?"

"Mmmm?"

"You won't ever . . . I mean . . . Was I alone? Did you feel *nothing*?"

"You weren't alone."

"But . . ."

"But what?"

"Jacques, I just gave you . . . I mean . . ." She could find no words to express her thoughts.

"This is part of life, one of your new experiences," he told her calmly. "There will be more. Moonlight and tropical sunsets."

"Vladimir was right!" She sat up angrily. "You are

cruel! This meant nothing to you! A challenge. A new filly to tame. I've seen trainers like you. They buy a horse nobody can handle, make her docile and obedient, then sell her for three times the price."

She pulled her clothes on quickly, feeling devastated and ashamed suddenly of her wanton nakedness. So this was the real world she'd read about—one-night stands, carefully calculated seductions. He had studied her carefully, building up her trust, finding all her weaknesses and playing unmercifully upon them. She should have recognized the kind of trainer he was. "I wish I'd never met you," she cried out, trying to hold back the tears as she fled out the door.

Chapter Eight

"I CAN'T CRY anymore," she gasped aloud as she leaned against the door to her room. There had been so many tears at Bud's death and over selling the farm and horses that she thought herself incapable of ever crying again. But those had been tears of grief and loss. Tears of this heartbreak and humiliation seemed to come from a different reservoir and flowed in torrents, quite as violently as the others.

Simone's carefully powdered face flashed menacingly before her eyes. Why hadn't she thought about that before making love to Jacques? She should have known that she couldn't compete with a woman who had produced a man's child.

But his words just before they made love had seemed so sincere. That loneliness she had always felt, her dependence on horses. Had he only used that as a lure—a hand held out with a carrot to a reluctant horse?

It was true—one could increase the value of a horse tremendously by training it, but not a woman, who lost value as she passed from one man to another seeking new thrills and sensations. It had all seemed very glamorous in her hazy travel-brochure fantasy, but the reality now shone with glaring clarity through the fantasy mist.

At least that part of her life had been simple with Bud. She had been so young, he had not even considered making love to her until the wedding night. She smiled when she remembered how frightened she had been, how she had kept her white bridal peignoir on all night, too modest to undress completely. And Bud had been too respectful to make demands.

Where had that girlish modesty gone, when she could shed her clothes so shamelessly after knowing a man for only two days? She undressed and studied herself in the long mirror of the armoire. Her nipples were crimson, her skin still glowing with the reflected fire of his passion. Was she imagining it, or did her body seem fuller and softer now, more voluptuous than it had ever been?

She trembled again as she remembered the intimate details of those hours. Never in all her years with Bud had she experienced sensations like that, nor had she even come close. How was it that a man she had lived with as a husband had barely stimulated her and a man who was little more than a stranger could arouse such torrential passions?

Was it love? Was that possible in such a short time?

There was a rapping at her door. She hurried to put on a bathrobe. "Ariane, I must talk to you," said Jacques. Her heart beat wildly as she opened the door.

"No. I don't want to talk. Leave me alone."

Jacques stood in the doorway, his thick black hair falling onto his forehead, his dark eyes gleaming with anger. "Why did you run off before I had a chance to talk to you?"

"I . . . I don't know." Ariane was feeling bombarded with conflicting, confusing emotions: passion, humiliation, jealousy over Simone. By all rights, she was the one who should be venting her anger at him, putting him on the defensive, but he had deftly managed to reverse the situation, making her feel like the penitent child.

"You were rude to leave like that."

"Rude?" she gasped, and straightened up to face him. "You make love to me and then make light of it . . . make some joke out of it . . . and you call *me* rude? Get out of here," she said, seething. "Go back to Simone and her *boeuf Bourguignon*. I'm sorry I took you away from her tonight."

He crossed the room in two swift steps and grabbed her wrists. Her bathrobe fell open, and she saw him take in her body at a glance. She held his fiery gaze without flinching. "A horse who's had only one owner quickly becomes spoiled," he said harshly.

"Only if the horse is treated well," she shot back. "I'm not used to being taken so casually."

"Oh, yes, all the passion your dear husband was able to arouse in you . . . a million capriole leaps . . ."

"Bud *loved* me . . ." Whether it had been true or not she had to believe it now, believe in the solidity of that part of her life. "His love was worth much more than any cheap carnival trick—" Her voice broke off as the tears began to flow down her cheeks. Nothing was certain in life. Not Bud's love, not Jacques, not even her ability to ride a horse.

"Of course he loved you, Ariane." Through her haze of tears she saw in Jacques's eyes a growing tenderness as his grip on her wrists lessened.

"He loved his horses, of course," she told him, "but there was never another woman. I never had to compete with someone else. With you there is a Russian girl and a woman with your child. And who knows how many others? To you it is all the same. You don't know what it it to have one special—" She was talking rapidly through small gasps and sobs, unaware of all that she was babbling.

"Ariane," he murmured, "if you would only stop crying and let me explain."

"Oh, you don't need to explain. I understand very well. I don't like it, but I understand."

"You don't!" His voice was harsh again.

She broke away from him. "Leave me alone. I don't need your explanations. I'm your employee, remember? Someone who works your horses for a few days. You don't owe me anything but a salary, and there is no reason for you to be in my bedroom."

"No one ever had a better reason to be in your bedroom,

Ariane." He was coming toward her.

"Don't touch me, Jacques. Don't ever touch me again. I cannot think when you do. Nothing makes any sense."

"*Eh bien*," he said with a weary sigh. "You will not listen to reason tonight. Perhaps in the light of day you will be able to see clearly. Anything I say to you now you want to twist to fit into some narrow preconception. *Dors bien, ma jolie Ariane.* Sleep well."

A night's sleep did not leave her feeling refreshed. She had troubling dreams that caused her to wake up several times in the night. In them everything flowed together: Bud, Jacques, Wicked Willie. Luckily she had only committed herself to Jacques for a few days. He would simply have to find another trainer to help him out. The emotional toll on her was too great. It had been a grave mistake to mix business and pleasure.

Now that she knew something of the routine in the Valbonne house, she could tell as soon as she saw the dining room table that Jacques had already finished breakfast. The napkin was out of the silver napkin ring, and there was no longer a cup and saucer nor a plate for the *tartines* at his place. Danielle's place was still set. It would probably be hours before she meandered downstairs.

The maid served her café au lait, and Ariane helped herself to the fresh *tartines*, covering pieces of bread with sweet butter and raspberry confiture. She looked out through the French doors. The sky was very low and swirling with thick gray clouds. The lush meadows were an iridescent emerald in the diffused light. It was a melancholy day and fit her mood. She was not looking forward to seeing Jacques and lingered until the last possible moment over her breakfast.

Fortunately there was a smartly dressed couple down at the stable discussing business with him. He introduced her. They were the owners of a large dapple-gray gelding that Jacques was training for the show. Jacques spoke to Ariane in a cold, businesslike voice. "Wicked Willie looks better today. After you wrap him, start with the horses you worked yesterday."

She nodded, relieved that Jacques was treating her with a certain professional coolness. She was not ready for another emotional scene.

Wicked Willie was glad to see her. The swelling in his hock was down far enough for her to take him for a walk. As they passed the couple outside the stable the woman's eyes widened. "When did you purchase this stallion, Jacques?"

"Ariane brought him from America."

"I thought you weren't interested in buying another stallion," said the man.

"I had no choice in the matter. My sister bought him in New York and had him shipped over."

The woman looked with renewed interest. She went up and patted the horse's nose. "He's very docile for a stud. Look how sweet-tempered he is, Henri."

Ariane wanted to say something but realized it wasn't her place. She no longer owned Willie.

"Good papers?" asked the man.

"The best. From the finest bloodlines in America, and he has won several *prix de dressage* over there."

"Let us know if you're interested in selling him." Henri spoke to Jacques in a quiet, businesslike tone. "Our prize stud is getting old. We were looking to keep one of the colts, but not one of them in the last year has been anything to rave about."

"He looks like he'd be a good pleasure horse, too," said the woman. "That's one thing our stud never was. How much would you want for him?"

Ariane's heart was pounding uncontrollably. She was staring so hard at Jacques she was sure she might bore a hole in him, but his eyes were on Willie.

"I'd have to ask my sister," he said noncommittally. "It's not up to me."

Ariane's mouth dropped open. How could he even consider selling Willie? She nearly burst into tears. Would this be Willie's life now, going from one owner to another, exploited as a stud, nobody stopping to give him the love and the attention he was used to? She led him back into his stall and buried her face in his silky mane. "I can't let him do this to you, Willie."

She marched out to talk to Jacques and, seeing that the people had left, said, "If you really want to get rid of Willie, I'll buy him back from you."

"What are *you* going to do with him?" he asked point-edly.

"Take him back to New York."

"That will be wonderful for his spavin, cooping him up again in a ship. The reason he developed hocks like that in the first place was lack of exercise. I don't suppose you've ridden him at all in months, have you?"

"Well, no," she admitted. After Bud's death she had not been able to.

"A horse like that needs to be exercised regularly, every day. A ballet dancer who did as much dancing as Willie did that night would have swollen ankles, too, if he had not exercised for months. What do you plan to do with him in New York? Have him spend the rest of his life on the end of a longe line?"

He was whipping at her most vulnerable spots—her love for Willie, her fear of riding. She lashed back at him angrily. "It will be better than him getting passed from owner to owner here in Europe. He's too good a horse to merit that kind of treatment. I sold him to Danielle because I thought he'd get a loving home. I was wrong. Now I want him back."

Jacques softened, backing off when he saw how deeply he had hurt her. "I'm not going to sell him, Ariane, though the Vanladims are fine people and Madame Vanladim treats her horses better than she treats her poor husband, Henri. It sounds to me what you really want to buy back is last night."

She flushed deeply; she could feel her hands tremble uncontrollably as she spoke. "For a man who would never beat a horse, you certainly don't hesitate to dig your spurs into a woman when the fancy strikes you."

He held her shoulders steady. "Ariane, will you be reasonable for a moment?"

She could barely speak. "Jacques, you had better find yourself another trainer. I'm through!" She turned swiftly on her heel to hide her tears and started back up toward the house.

Jacques came after her and grabbed her arm tightly. "You didn't want to talk last night, but we are going to have to talk this morning. I won't let you run off in this state."

"You can talk to me while I'm packing to leave. I'll take a train to Brussels and while I'm there make arrangements with my bank to have the money transferred to you."

"What money?"

"Whatever your asking price for Willie is. You don't think I'd leave here without him?"

Jacques took a deep breath. Ariane could see the muscles in his face grow taut; color was mounting on his high cheekbones and emerald sparks flashed from his eyes. Gripping her arm savagely, he wheeled her around and led her back to the stable.

"I've got the black mare saddled for you. We're going for a ride."

"I just quit, remember?" He ignored her comment.

As they rounded the corner she saw that the dapple-gray and the black mare were both saddled and standing at a hitching post.

"So you're still too frightened to ride a ten-year-old child's horse?" he taunted her.

Her eyes narrowed angrily at the implication. Without answering him, she tightened the cinch and put her left foot into the stirrup, swinging her right leg over.

Jacques was in his own saddle just as fast and heading

toward the meadow. "We're not going to the ring?" she asked.

"Not unless you're too scared to take that mare out in the open." He dared her with mocking eyes and broke into a trot.

She urged the mare into a slow canter to catch up. It was a smooth, rocking gait, and Ariane had no trouble passing Jacques. He let her get just beyond, then put his horse into a slightly faster pace.

Thoroughbreds, she knew, would instinctively want to race, having a competitive spirit bred into them. Ariane felt a surge of energy from the hind quarter of her mount, whose long neck stretched to keep up with Jacques's horse.

Jacques was grinning now, his white teeth gleaming. "The mare wants to race. Are you still frightened of her?"

She glared at him.

"Think she could beat this old gray?"

"I know what you're trying to do to me," she bit out. She knew he was taunting her with a dare, just as he had done the night before.

"Just past that clump of trees over there. I'll bet you a bottle of red wine that mare won't make it."

"You're on!" She gathered up her reins.

The horses sprinted out, gaining momentum as they broke into a full gallop. The cold wind slapped her face, ruffling out her long auburn hair. The heady scent of spring fields and wildflowers assaulted her senses as the powerful legs of the black mare raced below her. They were as one, locked together with the primal forces of nature—the wind, the earth, motion, and energy. Her knees clasped tightly to the horse's flanks, she rode as she had made love the night before, with wild joyful abandon.

They were already past the trees and still going. Jacques was laughing, heading toward some low hedges. The two horses leaped over them at the same time. Ariane savored the moment—the moment of flight. She caught a glimpse of Jacques out of the corner of her eye. He was feeling the same exciting sensation.

"Who won?" she asked breathlessly.

"You did, Ariane." He grinned. "You are indisputably the winner. Come on, I'll buy you that bottle of wine if you'll share it with me."

They turned down a narrow cobblestoned road. There were a few brown brick houses with stepped roofs; in one of them was a tiny store.

Jacques handed her the reins of the dapple-gray while he went in; he emerged a few seconds later with a bag. Mounting again, he led them down another quiet lane. "There's a twelfth-century deserted monastery nearby," he told her.

The old building was in ruins, but tall graceful trees were everywhere in the overgrown gardens.

He tied the horses so that they could graze on the tall grass and opened the bottle of wine under a tree. He also produced from the bag a carefully wrapped piece of ripe Brie cheese.

"It's awfully early in the day for wine," she said, taking a sip of it.

"We've been riding longer than you think. It's almost noon."

"How time flies when you're having fun," she said lightly.

"You *were* having fun, weren't you?" His green eyes were twinkling under the black lashes. Never had she seen his skin so flushed from the wind and hard riding.

"Okay, so you accomplished what you wanted."

"What is it you think I wanted?"

She took another sip of wine and broke off a piece of cheese. "You wanted me to realize that horses are still my life. You succeeded. I suppose I knew that all along. Nothing in the world surpasses what we just did." She sighed.

"Not even last night?"

She looked away from him. She had almost forgotten her humiliation. "Last night was a mistake," she said slowly. "I shouldn't have let it happen. I can only blame myself. Any man would have taken advantage of a situation like that."

"*What* situation?" he asked with annoyance.

"Oh, you know," she mumbled uncomfortably. "You figured me for a lonely widow who needed..."

"So that's all it was to you?" There was a cruel tone in his voice. "Stud service to help mend the grief-stricken widow?"

"Jacques, I..."

He looked out across the fields. "I thought you were angry because I made a teasing remark after we made love and then I was silent. Or perhaps because Simone troubled you. But none of those was the reason. You were shocked at yourself for that base yearning in you for a man's physical love. You needed someone for a night to take your husband's place."

If he only knew how guilty she felt later because she'd never felt those things in all her married years with Bud.... But her pride would not allow her to reveal that to Jacques. "I was hurt," she began shakily, then continued with some anger. "I haven't learned yet to be blasé about love affairs—like you are."

"You'll learn." He stood up abruptly. "You're off to a good start."

He mounted his horse, and she followed on the black mare. "We've got work to do...or are you quitting?"

"No, Jacques, I just thought..."

"It was a mistake for me to expect something more of you," he said roughly as they trotted down the lane. "From now on it will be strictly business. I wouldn't want you to think I was taking advantage of your widowhood."

They did not return to the house the same way they had come. Ariane saw now that there was a shorter, more direct route alongside the main road to Bruges.

Since they were silent the whole way back, she worked on the mare's lead changes simply to keep her mind occupied. By the time they had reached the house the mare was easily doing flying lead changes when she exerted only the slightest pressure with her calves.

"Ariane," he said heavily as they dismounted, "whatever has happened between us, I do respect your ability with horses. I couldn't help but admire what you did with the mare in just this short time. I need someone with your talent to help me out. Will you consider staying on?"

He looked at her with a warmth that made her body tingle. Would she ever be able to say no to him? She nodded. "I'll stay. But just for these few weeks."

"I'll pay you well, and I promise nothing like last night will happen again."

As she unsaddled the mare, she realized bleakly that the promise of another night like the last was really the *only* reason she was staying.

Still, being wanted for her equestrian abilities was better than not being wanted at all. The mare gave her an affectionate nudge, and she patted her neck fondly. Why weren't people as easy to get along with as horses?

She looked up just in time to see the white Mercedes coming up the drive. Pierre jumped out excitedly, and Simone followed at a much more deliberate pace, stopping before she got too close to the stable.

Jacques went up to greet her. "You are busy again tonight?" she asked him, her arms folded provocatively.

"I'm free tonight," he said quickly. "But don't cook. Let's go out somewhere and take Pierre."

Ariane felt as though the earth were swallowing her up, and she leaned against the mare for balance. Until that moment she did not know how deeply affected she was. The night before, she had known ecstasy and then humiliation at his hands. Now she was reeling under the shattering influence of jealousy.

Every instinct told her to flee, to run to Paris. Perhaps she could buy Willie back later. To stay at the Valbonne estate another minute with Jacques would be torture.

But then the very same instinct that made thoroughbreds

want to compete in a race held her steady. That powdered blond filly might have Pierre and a ten-year handicap on her, she thought angrily, but she'd never lost a single blue ribbon she'd ever gone after, and if Jacques Valbonne were the blue ribbon, she could have a go at him, too!

She straightened her back and began walking toward them, mustering all her courage. "*Bonjour, Simone*," she said in a clear voice.

"*Bonjour*," Simone said with less enthusiasm, then turned brightly to Jacques. "Shall I stay for lunch today?"

"Yes, do, *Maman*," Pierre piped in. "Let's stay for lunch."

"Of course," said Jacques, taking her arm. "I'll tell the maids to put on two more places."

At the sight of Jacques taking Simone's arm and Pierre grabbing his other hand Ariane gulped hard, but she kept her smile firmly in place. Nothing she had ever worked for had come easy. But the prizes *had* come. Jacques, she vowed, somehow would be hers.

Chapter Nine

ARIANE WORKED HARD the next week, devoting all her attention to the horses. The way to Jacques's heart, as it had been with Bud's, was through his horses, she reasoned. She was accomplishing near miracles with two of the young colts. Jacques had wanted to enter them in a halter class at the show but had not considered them ready. Yet after only a week of Ariane's constant attention they were walking straight and calmly alongside her, lining up squarely in place and behaving like angels. She had always felt it was the most fun to work with the little ones, to teach them manners. If they were started off correctly, as Willie had been, they could go on to accomplish anything.

Danielle kept up her dizzying pace of going out every night, never hesitating to include Ariane in all her plans. But the hours Danielle kept were impossible for a trainer, and Ariane did not care for the disco nightlife scene that Danielle seemed to crave.

Jacques, though pleased with her work, left the house each night, sometimes before dinner, sometimes after, returning no later than eleven o'clock when she would hear his footsteps come up the stairs and pass her door. If he could see light spilling out from under the door he would say softly *"Bonne nuit,"* and she would answer back, wondering fleetingly if he was waiting for an invitation to come in. She would not give it.

He had spent the entire week uttering no more than polite small talk and greetings to her: *"Bonjour," "Bonne nuit," "Comment ça va?"* He was lavish in his praise of her work, but there were no more compliments about her as a woman. He was keeping his promise to leave her alone.

The silent vow she had made to win his love was slowly crumbling out of futility. A few times she had tried to flirt, but he misread her mood, thinking only that she was being friendly. Or perhaps, she speculated, he was only trying to let her know that her attempt was useless.

Pierre, however, was much friendlier with her now that she no longer threatened Jacques's relationship with his mother.

She had given enough lessons to children to know how to win them over as well as teach them. She began working with Pierre in her spare time, giving him pointers. Basically, he was an excellent rider and just needed to be reminded of minor points, such as keeping his chin up and his heels down. Soon he was following her around, asking questions, helping her with the horses. And since she was more patient with him, he began to spend even more time with her than with Jacques.

One night after Jacques had left for the evening, she and Danielle sat down to dinner. Danielle was looking very melacholy that night, much the same as when she had heard from Vladimir.

"Your mad Russian called again?" asked Ariane.

"Ah, no. My love life is in disarray. But so it is always," Danielle said with a sigh. "Now it is my whole life."

"But you always seem to have such a wonderful time no matter what you do," said Ariane, who had come to appreciate Danielle's natural exuberance for living.

"But it is empty, vacant. I get up late every morning; I go to bed late every night. I have men who act like children. I could travel, but there is no place to go that I wouldn't have the same kind of life. At least here I have my own home. I am comfortable. How nice it would be to have a profession like you and Jacques have."

"You could," said Ariane quickly. "Jacques has told

me that you are an excellent rider and that you have the ability to be a trainer."

"I do not have the heart or the soul for it, though. To go over and over the same thing with a not very intelligent animal, it makes of me a completely mad person. I have not patience to work all day with animals. I become angry and they become nervous because they do not know why I am angry. So. *Fini!* That is no good." She leaned her head on her hand, her elbow planted on the dining room table, and toyed with her dinner. "I know I cannot go on much longer in this kind of life."

"How about getting married and having children? Any one of the fellows I've seen you with seems willing to die of love for you."

"But I do not die of love for any of them."

Ariane was determined to bring Danielle out of her mood. "How about a profession then," she continued. "Surely there is something you like to do. What did you study in school?"

"Mathematics. How I love numbers—so logical, so empty of nuances. There is no poetry in a number—so uncomplicated."

Ariane laughed. "Not for me! I barely made it through algebra. I think it's *wonderful* you like math! And this is the age of math and science, computers and—"

Danielle waved her fork in the negative. "No, I am not a scientist; I am not a computer."

Ariane considered the problem. Danielle was anything but a computer. Surely there was some solution for a bright, witty girl who was good at math. "Isn't there anything you always thought you'd like to try?"

Danielle's eyes took on a mischievous glow, and she put down her fork. "Do you promise not to tell Jacques? He would kill me if he knew."

Ariane looked at her with surprise. "What is it?"

"Do you remember the afternoon I ran out of the house with the newspaper? I was so afraid he would suspect."

"Suspect what?"

"Ariane," she spoke in almost a whisper. "I play the

commodities and stock markets, and I am *very* successful at it!"

Ariane's mouth dropped open. "But that's wonderful. Why don't you want anyone to know?"

"Mostly it is Jacques. He would tease me very terribly."

"But you tease him all the time. What's the difference?"

She thought about it. "I suppose you are right. It is something I have always loved very much. Papa taught me how to read the financial pages when I was a little girl. For me it was like the ABCs. I know all the codes for all the companies."

"Your father would be thrilled that you want to go into his business!" said Ariane excitedly. "After all, Jacques has no interest in it."

Danielle shook her head sadly. "You do not understand. Papa is very *ancien régime* when it comes to women. And in Europe, one still does not see very many women in business. Papa would be embarrassed. Jacques, yes, would make him proud. Me? No. But come, let me show you my secret office."

Ariane followed her upstairs and into her bedroom and watched Danielle open an antique rolltop desk. "I have my file cabinets downstairs in the basement; this is just some of what I have been doing with my broker in Bruges."

Ariane looked over the lists of names and numbers, but they could have been written in Egyptian hieroglyphs for all she understood of them. "I am impressed, but it is meaningless to me."

"I shall tell you then very quickly. I have made a lot of money just this month in U.S. soybean futures. It's very exciting. If I had my own office, really an office, I could cause miracles to happen."

Ariane made one more vain attempt to understand what Danielle was showing her, then her attention was drawn away by a letter in English on the desk top. The letterhead read "The London School of Economics."

"Isn't that where your father went to school?"

Danielle drew the letter out of Ariane's hand quickly. "Yes . . . I didn't mean for you to see that. But I must confide in you. I have not told anyone. I made my application there several months ago, and they have written to tell me that I am accepted."

"Danielle, there is the solution to all your problems! You must go. It will be a wonderful life—you'll be doing exactly what you've wanted to do—what you're so good at."

Danielle sat dejectedly on her bed. "I cannot decide, Ariane. Yes, I know it sounds very logical and easy, but to tell Jacques, to tell Papa. You cannot imagine what agony I go through. It is why I run out and dance every night of the week, because I cannot make up my mind. As soon as I decide yes, I go to London, I do not have the courage to tell them."

"I'm sure Jacques would support you," said Ariane carefully. "Why don't you ask him?"

She giggled. "He has no idea that this is my passion. You see, when we were little, he hated Papa's work. He was terrible in mathematics, and so he ridiculed it. Because I always looked up to him, I always agreed."

"You are *not* just Jacques's younger sister. You are a woman, Danielle, capable of making your own decisions. You do not approve of Simone, but he does not stop seeing her simply because you don't like her."

Danielle opened her blue eyes very wide and looked with sympathy at Ariane. "So sad you have been since you made love to Jacques. Why do you not again? I can see he is very sad, too."

"How did you know that we . . . ?" Ariane looked at her with astonishment.

She smiled. "I am not blind."

Ariane sighed. "I guess I behaved stupidly. But I really don't understand the protocol. I was only eighteen when I got married. There had never been anyone else in my life. At twenty-seven I should know how to act, but I don't. And Jacques isn't really like anyone I've ever met— except where horses are concerned, and then he, well, he reminds me of my late husband—his single-mindedness, I mean." Ariane continued, relieved to be able to speak finally about her feelings. "That frightens me—to be smitten again with a man who loves horses to the exclusion of everything else. And there is the question of Simone and Pierre. How can I compete with—"

Danielle waved away the suggestion that she could not compete with Simone. "I have a confession to make to you, Ariane," she said, meeting Ariane's brown eyes with a steady gaze. "I hope you will not be angry, but when I met you in New York and learned your situation, I thought immediately of my brother, how perfect you would be for each other. I bought Willie and asked you to bring him over only because I wanted you to meet and fall in love."

Ariane was shocked. "But that's like trying to play God." She was not pleased at the prospect of someone meddling with her fate.

"Please don't be angry. It was just after Simone came back here to Bruges, and I could see what she was trying to do to Jacques. I was so happy ten years ago when he decided not to marry her. My life would have been unbearable. It is very selfish of me, I admit. But I like you very much. I hope you and I will be friends, even if you do not end up marrying Jacques."

Ariane softened. How could anyone stay angry at Danielle with her earnest, sparkling blue eyes, topsy-turvy curls, and unruly freckles? She meant well. "I think you can dismiss the idea of Jacques and me marrying, but yes, you and I will be friends, I'm sure, for a long time. And if I ever earn a fortune, I'll have you invest it in soybeans for me!"

That night Ariane sat up in bed reading, until she realized she had been going over the same paragraph three times without understanding a word. All she could think about was what Danielle had said. One phrase in particular. "I can see *he* is very sad, too." Could it be that Jacques still wanted her?

She closed her eyes and recalled every detail of that night in the room in back of the stables, the firelight turning their sleek bodies golden as though their passion burned from the inside out. She remembered how secure she had felt resting her head on his broad chest, his coarse black hair matted from the dampness of their lovemaking, and how he continued to caress her long after they were finished. Bud had always rolled over abruptly after making love and fallen fast asleep, leaving her awake with all her doubts and questions.

She heard footsteps on the stairs and opened her eyes to look at the clock. It was a little after eleven o'clock. Her heart began to pound as she waited for Jacques's "*Bonne nuit*." But tonight he did not say it. Instead, he paused at her door. "Ariane," he called out softly. "Are you still awake?"

She cleared her throat. "Yes, Jacques."

"May I see you for a moment?"

She started to put on her bathrobe, then decided not to. Perhaps the sight of her in a nightgown...

She reached for the doorknob, then reconsidered and quickly threw her pale blue velour bathrobe over her shoulders. How foolish to be so very obvious.

"Is everything all right down at the stables?" she asked as she opened the door. With a sudden fright, she thought perhaps he had bad news to report about Willie.

"They're all fine. May I come in—or would you rather we talked downstairs?"

"No, come in. After all, we don't have to, I mean, it's not as though we..." Nothing she could think to say sounded right, so she halted in midsentence while he came in, leaving the door open as he did. Perhaps he only wanted to discuss the horses.

Against the window stood a large table, and next to that was a comfortable green armchair. Jacques sank down in the chair, and Ariane, not sure where to place herself, sat uncomfortably on the edge of the bed, waiting to hear what he had to say.

Since there was little light on his side of the room, dark shadows accentuated the sculptured planes of his face, the high cheekbones making the hollows of his cheeks seem dark, his eyes deeper set. From where she sat and studied him, his green eyes looked black. He seemed tired, she thought; or was he, as Danielle had suggested, "sad"? She longed to run across the room and throw her arms around his strong neck, tell him how much she wanted and needed him, but she sat primly on the edge of her bed, waiting.

He ran his fingers through his thick black hair and leaned back in the chair, his long powerful horseman's legs stretched out before him. Never before had she thought of the armchair being made for a woman until she saw Jacques's lean, masculine bulk strain to fit into it.

"It is hell living in the same house with you, Ariane," he began.

"I can leave any day," she said lightly.

"You would rather do that than share my bed?"

She had not expected him to be so direct. Was he a man utterly without gentle euphemism? But wasn't that what she had wanted him to say? Hadn't that thought been on her mind every second for the last week? What *did* she expect of him? To say he *loved* her? That he wanted to *marry* her? She had known Bud five years before they even kissed.

"Jacques!" She could no longer hold back her feelings. In two leaps she was across the room and on his lap, planting kisses in the hollow of his neck. "I can't pretend that I don't want you every minute of every day. It's been hell for me, too. Watching you work and ride, sitting across from you at the dining table, every moment wanting to reach out and touch you, feel your arms around me."

His arms wound tightly around her. He stroked her long auburn hair, kissed her forehead, her eager lips. "Ariane, you and I are like twins with one soul. We belong together—always together."

She wasn't sure how he worked so quickly, but he soon had her robe and nightgown off and was carrying her swiftly in his strong arms to the bed, veering only to kick shut the door to the room. He lowered her gently, murmuring her name as he slipped under the sheets, his weight causing the bed to creak. He stretched out beside her, and

she felt the warmth of his muscular body envelop her.
There was space to explore the magnificent length of him.
He found the hidden patches of silken skin on her body,
under her arms where her breasts began, the soft flesh of
her thighs. His touch sent shivers of passion coursing
through her veins.

Their heartbeats found a cadence as they rediscovered
each other. He nipped her lips like a playful colt while his
strong hands moved down her back, grasping at the round-
ness of her buttocks. He pulled her tightly against him.
As she tightened her legs around him, she saw herself
riding bareback across a fragrant green meadow at dawn.
There were dizzingly high hedges to fly over, higher and
higher, until the hooves ceased to touch ground and they
raced across the morning sky like Pegasus on the icy north
wind, faster and faster on beats of thunder, toward the
blinding fiery light of the morning sun.

All the tension of the past week seemed to have melted
away. As they worked horses in the ring the next day,
each gesture and glance took on a special meaning. No
longer did she avoid his gaze, and his eyes were always
on her. The horses quickly sensed the affection between
them and were eager to share in it. The harmony Jacques
and Ariane felt filled their day. Toward sunset she saddled
up the mare, and Jacques joined her on the dapple-gray.
They cantered together across the meadow, which was
darkening with blue shadows and filled with the songs of
crickets. Putting the horses at an even gait alongside each
other, they reached out and held hands, throwing back
their heads, laughing with the sheer joy of touching and
riding at the same time.

Ariane's joy shattered into fragments when the telephone rang after dinner that night. Jacques answered it,
then returned to her side and announced he was leaving.

"Where are you going?" asked Danielle.

Ariane held her breath.

"Over to Simone's for a while," he said evenly. "I'll

be back later." He kissed Ariane on the cheek, evidently unaware that all the color had left her face.

As the door closed, Ariane stared helplessly at Danielle, but it was Danielle who had large tears in her eyes; Ariane was too stunned to show the turbulent emotion she felt.

"I don't understand," said Danielle. "Everything seemed perfect today. What happened?"

Ariane could not speak. She shook her head and rushed down to the stable. Just being near Willie always made her feel better. She sat down on his wooden feeder and let the tears flow. Willie walked slowly over to her, his ears forward, dropping his massive head so that his large brown eyes were level with hers and she could see her unhappy reflection in them. Patting his silky cheek, she rested her head on his bony forehead. "How could I have ever considered selling you, Wicked Willie," she said, sighing. "What would I do without you?" He pulled back his head for a moment and studied her again, sniffing the tears that ran down her cheeks, then rubbing them away with his warm soft nose.

"How can I ever be truly miserable," she asked, "with such a dear friend as you?" She kissed Willie and scratched the spot on his shoulders that he liked. She walked down the row of stalls. Several of the horses knew her now and expected her to stop and then pat a nose, tousle a mane. One of the little colts she had been working poked his small head out and nickered loudly at her. She went into his stall and hugged him around his neck. "You funny little fellow. Someday you'll be every bit as nice as my Willie."

Much calmer after her visit to the stable, she thought that if she had learned one thing from this trip, it was how necessary horses were to her. Never again would she kid herself into thinking she could live without them.

She took a deep breath of the icy night air as she made her way back to the house. She liked Belgium, the town of Bruges, and the old Valbonne mansion. For a few hours the night before, she had imagined herself living there with Jacques, filling the house with the joyful shouts of their children. Odd how a few words, a phone call could shatter a beautiful dream.

The sound of a car coming up the driveway made her wheel quickly around. It was Jacques returning home. He got out of the car and walked toward her. "You were down to check the horses?" he asked, seeming pleased that she had taken it on herself to do what he usually did at that time of night.

Words would not come out of her throat, so she simply nodded. Did he expect her to act as though nothing had happened, that their whole lives had not been turned around by his visit to Simone?

"Everything all right down there?" he continued, slipping his arm around her and giving her a warm kiss on the cheek. She stiffened and pulled away from him.

"The horses may be fine," she said, seething, "but *I'm* not."

"What is the matter with you, may I ask?"

"You don't have any idea?"

"You're angry because I went over to Simone's tonight?"

"You say it as though it were nothing!"

They walked up to the terrace and entered the house through the glass doors.

"Ariane, I cannot stop things abruptly with Simone. She is having tremendous problems with Pierre, and she needs a lot of help right now. You'll have to be patient about that. Simone and I have known each other for a long time. Believe me, there is no physical intimacy between us anymore."

"Since when?" she asked suspiciously.

He checked his watch. "Let's see, it's been..." He smiled. "Come on, Ariane, you know I'm just teasing."

"I *don't* know, Jacques. I suppose I should have asked you to explain it all last night, but I was so happy just to be in your arms again. And I guess, in a way, I didn't want to know. But I can't go on in this horrible limbo any more."

"Simone and I have not made love since the day I told her ten years ago that I would not marry her."

"But why is she so possessive of you . . . and why do you continue to see her every night?"

"Simone has little self-confidence, Ariane, for all her beauty. She has always been dependent on someone, and for many years it was me. Telling her I didn't want to marry her upset her life and she rushed into a marriage— possibly because she was pregnant. That I do not know. Because I did not take any responsibility then, I feel some obligation now to help her through this bad time."

They walked upstairs together, and he entered her room without invitation, assuming he would be expected to stay. "It is very noble of you, Jacques, to be so concerned about her," she said with a steadiness she did not feel, "but I am not ready to share you with anyone, no matter how chaste a relationship it might be. And you're not doing Simone any great favor by being there to attend to her every need and problem. If she is getting a divorce, sooner or later she is going to have to function on her own."

"If it were only Simone," he said heavily and sank down in the green chair. "Every day I look at Pierre and wonder. There is so much about him that was like me at that age. The only father he has ever known is living it up in Paris at the moment, and whether or not Pierre is actually mine, he has come to look upon me as a father. It would rip his insides out to be suddenly cut off from me at this point."

"But, Jacques, why must being a friend to Pierre entail being with his mother so much?"

"Because I know Simone very well. If I break off with her, she will leave here immediately, taking Pierre with her. Money is no problem, and she will probably drag the poor child around with her to Juan-les-Pins, Formentor— all the fashionable resorts—leaving him with strange baby-sitters while she goes out looking for a new love."

Ariane closed her eyes and straightened her shoulders. "Last night you said you loved me, that you wanted me forever. Were those empty words?"

"No, I meant that." He sprang up and took her in his arms. "I want to marry you; I want us to build a life together here. Every day can be as beautiful as the one we shared today; every night like last night."

She pried herself loose from him and walked across the room. "I can't think clearly when you're holding me like that, Jacques," she said shakily, trying to regain her composure. "But I cannot be pitted against a ten-year-old boy, trying to figure out whose needs are greater, his or mine. Either you tell them both tomorrow how you feel about me, that you plan to marry me, or I pack my bags, take my Willie, and get out of your life forever."

"Ariane!" he pleaded. "Be reasonable. Give it time."

"You may be able to, but I cannot. I know the agony I went through tonight when you walked out the front door."

"I'm only asking for a *little* time."

"How much is a little?"

"A few days."

A few days was not unreasonable when considering an entire lifetime with someone. And she had no desire to hurt little Pierre. If Jacques could manage to accomplish the split with Simone without running the risk of hurting the child, it would be worth the effort.

"You agree, then?" Jacques took her in his arms again and hugged her tightly.

"I love you, Jacques. How could I not agree?"

"I'll begin laying the groundwork tomorrow, and then the next day, I'll tell them both. Now, you and I have some very important business." The look in his eyes made her melt inside. He pulled her down on the bed and covered her face with kisses.

While the sweet erotic flush of sensations flowed through her, some level of Ariane's consciousness sent out a warning signal, and she disentangled herself from him. "It's only a few days," she whispered. "Let's wait until then."

"What does my telling Simone and Pierre have to do with our enjoying the pleasure of each other right now?"

The danger warning blared in her ears like an air-raid signal, making her want to run for cover. She knew what had set it off. "I told you what I suffered tonight when you left. I could not go through that again. For the next two nights you are going to visit Simone. As much as I love you and want to believe you, I will be sitting on pins and needles every second you are gone, wondering if she won't win out in the end. And if she did . . ."

"It's ridiculous to even hint—"

"If she did," Ariane repeated evenly, "remembering what we've done here would be like a knife wound in my heart."

"We must trust each other! If there is no trust, we cannot expect to have a successful marriage."

She shook her head with determination. "After this, I shall never question you again."

"I see." He smiled suddenly and kissed her lightly on the lips. "The carrot before the horse," he said, laughing. "You will make sure that I don't put it off any longer."

She returned his smile. "I hadn't thought about it like that. It can't help but be a small spur in your side."

He lowered his green eyes, letting them linger over her body, and touched the tip of her breast with his fingers. "I'd call it a whip at my flanks."

As she lay in her bed alone that night staring up at the dark ceiling, she regretted having put Jacques off. Every nerve in her eager body was screaming out to be caressed by him. Knowing that he slept alone just up the long hallway was a tremendous temptation. Only the thought of Simone kept her at bay.

For the time being, Jacques's love at a distance would keep her warm and content.

Chapter Ten

EARLY THE NEXT morning she was awakened by his footsteps in the hall. He paused at her door, then entered. "Don't ask me how, but I knew you were awake," he said, sitting on the edge of her bed. "I just wanted to see your beautiful auburn hair spread out like a halo on the pillow and kiss your sleepy lips. I missed you last night."

"Oh, Jacques, I missed you, too." She encircled his neck.

"I made a decision. I'm going to tell Simone today. Putting it off will only make it harder. I'm going to work a few horses, have breakfast, then drive over there."

She hummed happily around the stable after Jacques drove off to Simone's. When Danielle came down to the stable, she told her what Jacques was doing.

"Hallelujah!" She hugged Ariane. "Oh, just knowing that Jacques has the courage to tell Simone and Pierre gives me the courage to tell Papa that I am going to the London School! He arrives in Paris today from Copenhagen and is sending his jet to pick me up tomorrow. I told him that I had some very serious business to discuss with him. I am so nervous, Ariane, but there will be such happy news, too. You and Jacques together! How smart I was to introduce you, no?"

When Jacques returned they were still chattering happily to one another. They broke off abruptly and turned questioning faces to Jacques.

"Everything is fine," he said. "It was not easy, but I

should have done this months ago, even before you came, Ariane. What I didn't know, was that Simone all this time was considering going back to her husband. She did not want to hurt me. It was a good confession all around." He laughed. "And probably it is best for Pierre to return to the father he has known and loved all his life."

The three went arm in arm back to the house for luncheon. Danielle opened a bottle of champagne to celebrate the engagement and kissed them both. "Now, as long as this is the day for confessions," she said, straightening her shoulders and winking at Ariane, "I have a confession to make to Jacques."

"Don't tell me." He grinned. "I already know."

"You do?"

"Yes, that you only bought Wicked Willie to make sure I met Ariane."

"You told him?" she asked Ariane.

"No." The two young women looked at him in surprise.

"I know my mischievous sister pretty well." He grinned.

"Not so well as you think," said Ariane, giving an encouraging look to Danielle.

"You're not marrying Vladimir?" he asked with mock horror.

"No."

"Popeye?"

"Marry Christiaan—are you crazy? I would marry Vladimir and start a Bolshevik revolution in the canals of Bruges before I took on the Dutch navy."

"Albert?"

"No."

"Bernard?"

"No."

"Then what are you confessing?"

Danielle bit her lower lip, then blurted out her news.

"The London School of Economics?" Jacques paused a moment to let it sink in, then jumped up from the table and ran to hug her. "What a wonderful idea! You've always been so good with numbers, and you loved Papa's work. Why didn't you think of it before?"

She wrinkled her button nose happily. "Then you don't think it's silly?"

"Danielle, I have accused you of doing many frivolous and crazy things, but this is definitely not one of them. This is the sanest thing you've ever done. We'll miss you while you're in London, but London isn't that far. We can visit back and forth."

"Jacques, what do you think Papa will say?"

"He'll be thrilled, of course."

"I hope you're right." She shuddered.

"Now I have a confession to make to Ariane," said Jacques suddenly with a mischievous grin, "since this is to be a day of candor and confessions. It's about Willie."

"What about Willie?" asked Ariane with surprise.

Danielle beamed. "I didn't tell her. Never in my life have I kept a secret so well, Jacques."

"Your treatment for bog spavin. We've had it in Europe for years. I use it frequently."

Ariane looked at him in shock. "Then you never did plan to give him a shot of cortisone?"

"Not at first, but that one morning when his hock seemed to be worse, I considered it seriously."

"But if you knew about the ointment, why didn't you tell me?"

"I wanted to keep you here."

She looked from Danielle to Jacques and burst into a wide smile. "This was a conspiracy from the beginning. And I've never been happier." She rushed to throw her arms around Jacques and kissed him hard several times before resting her head on his chest. Suddenly her joy was pierced. "Did Pierre really understand?"

"It's hard to tell with children—but he seemed to accept it." He pulled back, looking down into her face with tenderness. "I told him that I wanted him to come over here often, maybe even spend a month during the summer— that is, if you don't mind."

"He and I have gotten to be very good friends this last week." She smiled. "I'd be delighted."

"He'll be over here this afternoon as usual, so we'll get a better idea of how he's taking it and what to do."

When Pierre arrived, Ariane did not notice any change in him. He acted as though nothing monumental had transpired. She had expected some resentment, but perhaps the prospect of his mother and father in Paris getting back together had smoothed over any ruffled feelings. She decided to talk to him that afternoon, believing that it was always better with children to bring things out in the open and quickly.

During his riding lesson, she complimented him profusely, as he was doing everything she had taught him without being reminded. While they walked the horse out after the lesson she said, "I'm glad we're friends, Pierre. At first I didn't think you were going to like me very much."

He smiled and scuffed his feet, as little boys all over the world do when they're shy or embarrassed. "I think you're very nice, and you don't yell so much at me when you give me a lesson like Jacques does."

"He yells at you?"

"Well, maybe not really yells, but he does not have as much patience as you do."

"I thought maybe you didn't like me because you thought I might take Jacques's affection away from you," she said, launching into the subject. "I would never do that, and Jacques loves you very much."

"Jacques came to talk to *Maman* and me about that this morning," said Pierre with a knowing smile.

"I'm glad you understand." She put a tender hand on his shoulder.

"I always knew that *Maman* and Jacques would get married," continued Pierre.

"What?" She wasn't sure she'd heard him correctly.

"Jacques said this morning that he was going to marry

Maman, just like she said he would. She and I are going to come live here in this house with him and I will have my own horse, not the black mare, but a brand-new one that I can ride in shows with Jacques. He is going to be my father now."

"Pierre, I think you must have misunderstood . . ." She was on shaky ground and knew it. Either he was believing only what he wanted to believe, living in a fantasy world, or Jacques had been lying to her. Neither prospect was pleasant.

"Jacques did not talk about me?" she asked tentatively.

"Yes. He said that he was being nice to you for the next week because you were helping him with the horses, then you were going to take your Wicked Willie and go back to America."

She gulped. This was a little boy full of fantasies, she tried to tell herself. Jacques was coming toward them. She had to think quickly how to handle the situation.

"How'd you ride today?" Jacques asked Pierre.

"He did splendidly," Ariane said quickly. "I didn't have to remind him once to keep his heels down or his knees in. We were just having an interesting discussion. Pierre, tell Jacques what you were just saying to me."

Pierre did not flinch or look at the ground as though he might have been caught in a lie but gazed directly at Jacques. "I just told her what you said this morning."

Jacques smiled. "Good. I'm glad you two have come to an understanding."

"I'm sorry, Jacques," the boy said quickly. "But I told her the truth. What you told me *not* to tell her."

Jacques's expression became quizzical. "Pierre?" He kneeled down to put himself at eye level with the child. "What is all this you're saying?"

"I told her the truth, not the lie you told me to tell her."

"Pierre," he said sternly. "What did you tell Ariane?"

"That you and *Maman* are going to be married, and we are going to live here and you are going to buy me a new horse and Ariane is going to leave here in a week right after the show in Brussels."

"Pierre, you tell Ariane the *truth*," he said angrily. "Or we will never be friends again."

"That *is* the truth!" cried Pierre. "You wanted me to lie to Ariane, but I won't do it! I won't do it! She has been very nice to me. I won't lie to her!"

He ran off and Ariane started after him, but Jacques held her back.

"I expected some trouble, but not this. He's completely lost his hold on reality."

"But shouldn't you go talk to him?"

"No, let him run home. It isn't far. He knows what he's done. It will be best to let him come around."

Ariane had a squeamish feeling in the pit of her stomach. The trouble was that Pierre's lies had a frightening ring of credibility to them. Could a ten-year-old manage to create such a convincing lie? Jacques did need her desperately to get those horses ready for Brussels. She had been a godsend to him. There were several horses along with the two colts which he had not even considered showing until she worked with them.

If her husband had not been above marrying her to exploit her talents, why should Jacques be any different? Perhaps he wouldn't go so far as to marry her, only seduce her, convincing her of his love—and all to keep her there and happy until after the international exhibition.

Why couldn't he have been reassuring Simone that morning that he would marry her if she would just be understanding for a few more days—just until after the show? Hadn't he asked *her* to be patient? Just a few more days?

As hard as she tried to rid herself of this malignant theory, it kept coming back with increasing force.

At four o'clock she and Jacques paused for a cup of coffee and *tartines*. It was one of the Belgian rituals that she enjoyed most. A maid brought a tray down to the stable; they sat on the patio outside the stable master's red room, where she and Jacques had first made love.

Thoughts of that night in his arms floated back to her as she watched his lips on the coffee cup, but the thoughts were not enough to obscure what Pierre had said.

"You still worrying about Pierre?" asked Jacques.

She nodded.

"So am I," he said quietly.

When the maid reappeared to clear the tray, she announced, "Monsieur Jacques, Madame Simone just called and said you must come to her house right away. It is very important."

He leaned over to kiss Ariane. "I don't know how long I'll be. Will you take Xenophon, the big brown gelding, over the five-foot fence for me? And Le Roi Soleil, the bay stud, needs some work on his transition from trot to passage."

She nodded. Of course she would do it. She watched him rush off. Was he going to reassure Simone that he still meant to marry her—that Pierre had betrayed them? Had Pierre actually been doing her a favor by giving her fair warning?

She felt an icy chill, remembering what the crazy Dmitry had said about Jacques. She had not believed him, having been too enamored of Jacques to think him capable of treating a girl callously, cruelly. But hadn't he also left Simone suddenly many years before—even while she was possibly pregnant with his child?

Ariane went through the motions of working the horses, but her heart wasn't in it. Each time she thought she heard a car drive up, her heart jumped. Danielle had gone to Zeebrugge to shop for clothes and have dinner with some friends, so Ariane was alone in the house. When she returned for dinner, one of the maids informed her someone had called to leave a message that Jacques would not be home for some time and for her to go ahead and eat without him.

"Did they say when he'd be back?"

"No, madame."

"Was it a man or woman who called?"

"A woman, madame."

"Did she leave a phone number where he could be reached?"

"No, madame. Would you prefer your dinner in the dining room or in the study in front of the television?"

At least the television would be some company, she thought, better than sitting in the huge dining room alone.

She could barely touch her dinner, wondering when Jacques would return home or at least call. It was about ten when the telephone rang, the sound jarring her. A maid picked it up before she could answer, then buzzed the study on the intercom. "Monsieur Valbonne wishes to speak to you," she said.

Ariane breathed easier knowing Jacques was on the line and hastened to pick it up.

"Bon soir, Ariane. Ça va?"

It was Monsieur Valbonne all right—but not the one whose voice she so desperately wanted to hear. It was Jacques's father. She tried to mask her disappointment. "Hello, yes, I'm fine. Neither Jacques nor Danielle is here at the moment."

"How ill-mannered are my children for leaving you alone. Jacques is at Simone's, I imagine."

"Yes." She wondered if he could detect the agony in her voice.

"And Danielle is dancing in Zeebrugge with her *co-pains.*"

"You know your children very well." Ariane forced a weak laugh.

"It was very kind of you to stay and help Jacques with the horses. This show means a great deal to him. He works very hard for it every year."

"I'm happy I can help out."

"You are enjoying Bruges?"

"Yes. It's a beautiful city, and your house here in Sainte-Croix is also lovely."

"When are you coming to Paris?"

"I'm not sure—soon, I hope."

"Why not come tomorrow with Danielle? I'm sending my jet to pick her up. Surely Jacques will give you the day off. Didn't you say you had an aunt here?"

"Yes, I've spoken to her several times."

"Good. Well, then, I hope to see you tomorrow."

"I'm not sure I can get away, that is, if Jacques..."

"Oh, I know Jacques before a major horse show! He thinks of nothing else. He will work you to death if you're not careful. You mustn't let him take advantage of your kindness. Well, I won't keep you. Please tell Danielle that the plane will be there at ten ten o'clock and I have reserved her favorite corner table at Tour d'Argent for lunch. I hope I'll have the pleasure of seeing you there, too."

By eleven o'clock Jacques had still not called. She walked down to the stable to check on the horses, hoping Jacques would be at the house when she returned, but he wasn't. Leaving Monsieur Valbonne's message at Danielle's door, she changed into her nightgown.

It was impossible to sleep. At every little sound she almost jumped out of her skin. It was too late for Jacques to call her now.

Shortly after midnight she heard a car drive up and listened hard for footsteps. They were unmistakably the light, breezy steps of Danielle.

For a moment Ariane debated getting out of bed to talk to Danielle, but then decided against it.

When morning finally came, she dressed quickly and went down the hall to Jacques's room. It was empty, the bed neat as a pin, obviously unslept in. Her heart raced. Tears misted her eyes. She wheeled, then raced through the house and out to the stables. There was no sign of Jacques. Mechanically, she put out feed and water for the horses.

She was dazed with pain. Staying all night with Simone—what a cruel way for Jacques to confirm her worst fears about his sincerity. But why now, a week before the show, instead of the day after it started? Simone. She'd probably put her foot down on Jacques's charade.

Ariane's stomach knotted. She found Willie and held him tightly around the neck.

She applied the special ointment to Willie's hock one last time. It was almost completely healed and really didn't need another treatment. "I won't leave you here for long," she whispered. "Just as soon as I get things straightened out in Paris I'll send for you, and we'll go home to New York."

It was eight o'clock by the time she rushed back up to the house to change and pack. Danielle was wandering downstairs sleepily when she came through the French doors.

"How you exist at this hour is beyond me," mumbled Danielle, rubbing her eyes. "I've got to pull myself together to get to Papa's plane."

"I'm going with you," said Ariane quickly.

"You're what?"

Ariane explained what had happened the night before. Danielle kept shaking her head. "I cannot believe that Jacques would play such a horrible trick. I don't like this, not at all."

Ariane experienced only one moment of doubt about her decision. As she put her suitcase into the trunk of Danielle's car she glanced up at Jacques's window. Danielle noticed it.

"Please, Ariane, leave a note for Jacques. Tell him where you have gone and why. Ask him to explain. You will never be able to live with yourself if you don't. He must be given a chance."

"No," she said decisively, slamming down the trunk door.

As they sped down the lane she fought a desire to look back at the house, then with a sudden impulse looked over her shoulder. The heavy Flemish clouds were hanging ominously low over the house.

Chapter Eleven

SINCE SHE HAD given herself no time to contact her aunt before she left Bruges, Ariane went with Danielle to the Hotel George V to call.

"Ariane! I was just about to call you in Bruges." *Tante* Yvette sounded as though she were in a hurry. "I'm running to catch a train to Nice. Uncle Louis's mother is very ill, and we are afraid she will not last many more days. I didn't expect you here for another week. But never mind, I shall leave a key with our concierge and she will show you where everything is. You can find your way easily on the metro. Take the Sèvres line and get off at Michel-Ange Molitor."

"I have the address, Tante Yvette, and I can have the Valbonnes' chauffeur drop me off."

"Their *chauffeur*? Oh, *mon dieu*! Where are you now?"

"The Hotel George V."

"George V? *Mon dieu!*"

She knew why her aunt was impressed. She was standing in a rococo room with pale blue walls and intricate gold-and-white molding that would have suited Marie Antoinette perfectly.

Danielle suggested she stay there with them instead of going to her aunt's. "After all, it is a three-bedroom suite. Papa keeps it all the time for when Jacques and I both come to town. One bedroom will be empty. It would be a pity for you to go to your aunt's apartment and be all alone."

It took Ariane only a few seconds to consider and accept the offer. The fact was she couldn't bear even the thought of being alone in so miserably sad a state.

"Besides," Danielle added, "we can have Papa's chauffeur take us around sightseeing while he is in meetings." Danielle was eager for Ariane's support at lunch when she broke the news about her plans to her father.

After a breathtaking tour of the elegant city, so different from Bruges, the two met Danielle's father at the Tour d'Argent, an elegant restaurant known to be the most expensive in Paris. Ariane, still not used to the tremendous wealth of the family, noted that Monsieur Valbonne seemed unaware of the exorbitant prices of the items on the menu.

Obviously delighted to see Danielle, he made her promise to spend a few days in Paris. "In my hectic life," he explained to Ariane, "I have not always had time to go to my children, so whenever I can I have tried to bring them to me. My pilot, I'm afraid, has had a busier life than he might have. When Danielle and Jacques were younger, I used to send for them almost every weekend, and they would arrive with a harried maid who was always on the verge of quitting."

"Jacques and I were not, you might say, model children," said Danielle, laughing. "Do you remember that prune-faced Austrian woman who forbade us to eat sweets? We used to secretly get on the telephone and order chocolate pastries from room service every few minutes, then when they'd arrive, pretend we didn't know anything about it."

The mention of Jacques, even as a little boy, made Ariane's heart jump. She wished she had known him then, naughty though he might have been. He must have looked very much like Pierre. She wondered again about Pierre. Could he have been lying, after all, playing the naughty little boy? But the cold fact remained—Jacques had spent the night with Simone.

She was brought quickly back to the present when she felt Danielle nudge her under the table. It was time for Danielle to speak to her father about the London School.

"Oh Papa," she began. "Ariane and I had such a lovely time this morning. We walked up the Champs Élysées, so I was lucky enough to see the expression on her face the first time she saw the Arc de Triomphe! And we went past Madame Monique's dress shop."

"Chez Monique!" exclaimed Monsieur Valbonne. "That was one of your mother's favorite shops. But I thought she would surely close when her husband Philippe died. After all, she was able to create those beautiful gowns only because a masculine eye watched over all her expenses."

"Well, someone is still watching over them, *cher* Papa," continued Danielle, her eyes taking on a serious look. "Her daughter Annick. A professional accountant."

Ariane, afraid that Danielle would become too angry at her father's remark to present her plans for her future persuasively, quickly spoke up. "Yes," she added. "It's marvelous that so many women have trained for practical professions nowadays."

"Perhaps for women like you, Ariane," commented Monsieur Valbonne, "whose profession is horses. That is a profession you can and did share with a husband. But I see these faceless women in their masculine suits trying to compete with men in money matters."

Danielle shot Ariane a look of despair.

"There are, Monsieur Valbonne," countered Ariane, "many men in my profession who think women are not strong enough to deal with horses. I always tell them that it takes patience and intelligence, not brute force, to work with animals. But I cannot think of any reason a woman would not be equipped to handle money matters. What kind of strength does it take to wield a pencil across an accounting sheet?"

He laughed, delighted at her reasoning. "How clever

a girl you are! You are right. I am very old-fashioned, but one must be reasonable. When I was at the London School of Economics, I remember students from old families who were upset to see young men from the middle classes studying there. But things had to change." Yet just when they seemed to have gotten Monsieur Valbonne in the right mood to discuss Danielle's future, his attention was caught by something across the room.

"Danielle," he asked, "isn't that Jean-Paul Molinard sitting alone at that table?"

Both Ariane and Danielle looked quickly in the direction he indicated. Ariane drew in her breath. If she had not known that Jacques was in Bruges, she would have sworn that the man seated alone near the far wall was the Belgian aristocrat. So this was Simone's estranged husband!

"He's alone," continued Monsieur Valbonne. "We should invite him over."

"Oh, Papa," sighed Danielle. "He's only slightly more insufferable than his wife."

But Monsieur Valbonne was firm. "Papa, you are so rigid in your etiquette." Danielle spoke wistfully, knowing that all hopes of raising the matter of her plans were dashed.

"What is thoughtful is never rigid; it is correct," he said in such a way as to stifle any further argument from his daughter, then went over to Jean-Paul Molinard's table.

"Now I won't have a chance to tell Papa about the school," she whispered desperately to Ariane.

"Yes you will—you'll just have to do it later. Don't worry because I won't be there, Danielle. You were strong enough to apply and to be accepted on your own merits. You really don't need my support to tell him." She hoped the look in her eyes and the tone of her voice matched the optimism of her words.

The men seated themselves at the table, Jean-Paul obviously grateful to be included in their party. He immediately set his eyes on Ariane, who stiffly put him off.

Miserable as she was about Jacques, she was in no condition to carry on a flirtation. And Jean-Paul was, as Danielle suggested, the male counterpart to his estranged wife. Another century would have mercilessly labeled him a fop or a dandy. There was something too perfect in his styled hair, his manicured nails, and his silk shirt.

What continued to surprise Ariane most, however, was the outward resemblance to the horseman. If Simone had gone through a photo catalog and picked out a face to match her lost love's she could have come no closer. The features and coloring were remarkably similar, down to the green eyes.

Had he not opened his mouth to speak, Ariane might have found herself attracted to him for the same reasons Simone had been. But nothing in their personalities bore even the slightest similarity. She was certain that Simone, with her shallow preoccupation with appearances, had not even noticed how utterly without character this man was.

Jean-Paul placed a cigarette in a gold holder and lit it with a flourish.

"It all began at a party in Cannes," he began when Danielle asked him pointedly why he and Simone were getting a divorce. "The truth is one should never go to Cannes off-season. All the wrong people are there. And the weather is not agreeable. Well, who do you suppose I should see there?" He paused.

"Don't keep us in suspense," said Danielle dryly.

"Hélène Pélisier!"

"Please, Jean-Paul, who is Hélène Pélisier?" asked Monsieur Valbonne, his usual civility strained to the limit by Jean-Paul's roundabout way of speaking.

"Don't you remember her? She was in all the papers that year. *Paris Match* did an entire article on her, and there was a picture of us both with Princess Grace in Monaco. She gave us a party, you know, to celebrate our engagement. *Jours de France* had the story and some photos of Hélène in front of her father's château. It was Hélène, you know, who broke the engagement to marry an Italian painter. *Quel scandale!* But then I met Simone. Ah, Simone." He lifted his eyes to heaven.

"Jean-Paul, all you have said is that you saw Hélène Pélisier again," said Danielle impatiently. "That could not be enough to make you divorce Simone, unless—"

"Oh, no! Between me and Hélène it was finished, but you can imagine we had many things to talk about, friends in common. Hélène still looked very beautiful in a long Dior gown that was emerald-green—you have seen the kind of gown which has no back at all? And Hélène had a marvelous tan because she had just been for two weeks on a yacht in Rio. It was a very striking effect, the green dress against the tan. It would have been impossible not to notice. Everyone at the party commented on it. But when I said something, Simone flew into a rage."

"Jean-Paul, do you mean to say that you and Simone are getting a divorce over a green dress?" asked Danielle.

He sighed. "The green dress was only the beginning. There was an ugly argument in front of everyone that was quite embarrassing to me. Simone left the party early, but I stayed at the house for a long time. Well, if you would like the absolute truth . . ."

"By all means, Jean-Paul," said Danielle.

"I stayed at the party all night. And then I invited Hélène to breakfast with me. We were sitting at a table outside—you know that charming little Café Rosetta on the Croisette near the Hotel Carlton where the croissants are quite the best on the entire Côte. In that climate, as you well know, they can be quite heavy if extreme care is not taken."

Ariane was amazed that a man on the brink of losing his wife would worry about heavy croissants.

"I should have realized that the Café Rosetta was where Simone liked to breakfast, too. But it was still a shock to see her and little Pierre there. Of course she assumed that I had spent the night with Hélène."

"And you didn't?" asked Danielle.

"*Je t'en prie*, Danielle!" admonished Monsieur Valbonne, who clearly was not interested in such intimate details.

"We were at the same party all night, but we did not sleep together."

Monsieur Valbonne relaxed.

"I explained this to Simone and so did Hélène Pélisier. But she would not believe either of us. The next thing I knew she was back in Bruges. I call every single day, but she will not speak to me. Finally she told me she was seeing *her* ex-boyfriend."

Everyone at the table suddenly came alert.

"Need I say to whom she was referring?" He took a final drag from his cigarette and extinguished it slowly, every move deliberate, as if the attention of his entire being was necessary to perform the simple act.

Ariane felt a little sorry for him as she watched that gesture. Insipid and ridiculous as he was, Jean-Paul had obviously been badly hurt.

"She . . . she said that she had always loved Jacques and that she had only married me because . . . because I looked so much like him." His voice was cracking now with real emotion; his green eyes were moist. "And she said she was going to marry him as soon as our divorce was final. She even said that he wanted to . . . to . . ." He had to take a sip of wine before he could complete the sentence. ". . . to adopt Pierre." His hand was trembling as he lifted the glass again to his lips. "I could give her a divorce, though it is the last thing in the world I want, but never could I give up Pierre. Oh, I know there was some question." He looked down at his plate with his untouched lunch still on it. "But Pierre is *my* son. I am the one who has been a father to him, and I have given him all the love a father has. We have always been very close, Pierre and I. Every Sunday I took him to the Parc Monceau and every night I read to him. I sit in his room in Paris—with his books and his toys—and I think about his laughter . . ." He paused and looked up at all of them sadly. "How indulgent you are to listen to the recitation of my problems."

Monsieur Valbonne was the first to pull himself together, as they had all been affected. "It is necessary to
talk sometimes, Jean-Paul."

As sympathetic as Ariane felt, she could not stop her
own anger as she heard in his sad confession a confirmation
of everything she now believed to be true of Jacques.
Pierre must have been telling the truth, after all. Jacques
planned to marry Simone and adopt the child. The only
reason Jacques could have had for playing her along was
his need for someone to help with his horses.

Jean-Paul pushed some food around his plate without
taking a bite. "Yesterday, it was very odd, but Simone
called me."

Danielle quickly jumped in. "Maybe she has changed
her mind and she wants you back?"

"Whatever she wants, I no longer care."

"But what did Simone say?" Danielle asked. Ariane
was now regarding him with intense interest. In spite of
all the evidence, she still clung to a glimmer of hope that
Simone's story of marrying Jacques was all an elaborate
hoax to get even with her husband.

"It's of no importance."

"But after all this time when she wouldn't talk to you,
it must have been of some significance, eh?" Danielle
pressed him.

He shrugged. "I do not have any idea what she wanted
to say, because I told my maid to say that I would not talk
to her. It is now her turn to suffer my silence." He smiled
faintly. "Do you know that she even had the nerve to tell
the maid that it was an emergency?"

Monsieur Valbonne looked at him gravely. "But Jean-
Paul, what if it *is* an emergency?"

"Bah! She is lying. I called her many times and said
it was an emergency. But do you know what she had her
maid tell me?" He drew himself up. "She said that she
would not come to my aid if I were dying in the street."

"I'm sure she did not mean that," said Monsieur Valbonne, his eyes wide. Jean-Paul's entire recitation had
made him uncomfortable. He was reasonable, well-orga-

nized, and tidy in his affairs, a man who held his belief in good manners with the fervent conviction of a priest. This display of childish behavior was not to his taste, and he deeply regretted the role his son was playing in the intrigue.

"There are wonderful pastries for dessert here," he said to Ariane to change the subject.

"Ah, you must try the chocolate éclairs," said Jean-Paul enthusiastically, seeming to forget his troubles. "They are perhaps the best in all of France, though there is a splendid *pâtisserie* in Avignon. Have you been to visit Avignon? That part of France is quite agreeable this time of year. If you are going to the Côte, you must go through Avignon."

Ariane was amazed at how quickly he had dropped the painful subject of Simone and embarked on a gourmet's tour of France for her. And however distressing his marital problems were, they did not prevent him from taking her aside after lunch as they were waiting for Monsieur Valbonne's chauffeur. "You are the most beautiful woman in Paris," he whispered ardently. "I *must* see you. When can we meet?"

"I am very busy with the Valbonnes," she said as coldly as possible, shrinking back from him. "Then I am going to stay with my aunt here in Paris."

"Then I can see you at the house of your aunt."

"Well, I don't think—"

"Where does she live?"

"In the sixteenth arrondissement, but—"

"I also live in the sixteenth. Which street?"

"Rue de Civry, but Jean-Paul—"

"What luck! I am just around the corner. We must be neighbors. What number?"

"I . . . I can't remember." Not wishing to be rude, she hoped the *chauffeur* would hurry so she would not have to reveal any more.

"Then what is your aunt's name? I shall use the phone book."

Just then the chauffeured limousine appeared, and Ariane was quick to be the first in, sliding to the far end of the car so that she would be furthest from the curb. But Jean-Paul was quicker than she imagined and in seconds had circled the car and was at her window. "Please, what is your aunt's name?"

"Mangin," she mumbled, hoping he didn't hear correctly, but he had a pencil in hand and was scribbling down the information he had gleaned in a tiny black address book as the limousine pulled into the street.

"You're not planning to see him, are you?" Danielle looked at her with horror.

"Oh, no! But I didn't know how to be polite and not give him my aunt's name."

"Jean-Paul Molinard is a man who does not understand subtlety, Ariane. With that kind of ignorance, one must be very direct," advised Danielle. "You must say, 'Jean-Paul, go drown yourself in the Seine.' Or 'Jean-Paul, *mon cher*, go leap off the Tour Eiffel.'"

"Danielle," said her father with a frown.

"Well, Papa, there is no other way for Ariane to be rid of such a pest. How did Simone put up with that for ten long years?"

"Perhaps, *ma fille*," he said with a wry smile, "Simone did not notice."

"Oh, Papa." Danielle giggled. "I think you are finally to understand what I have been saying about Simone for so many years!"

He closed his eyes thoughtfully for a moment. "After hearing this today, I admit that I have not very much regard left for either Simone or Jean-Paul Molinard. I have pity for the child, Pierre. What a shame a child cannot choose his parents."

"If I had a choice, Papa, I would always choose you." Danielle gave him an affectionate hug.

That afternoon as she and Danielle continued their tour of Paris, Ariane almost envied Jean-Paul Molinard the ease

with which he had temporarily forgotten Simone in his
silly infatuation with her. Nothing she saw in the exquisite
city was a powerful enough antidote to make her forget
Jacques—even for a second.

Chapter Twelve

WHEN THEY ARRIVED back at the hotel, Danielle made Ariane sit down and placed a glass of Courvoisier in her hand. *"Assez!* Enough! You are suffering too much. I am going to call Jacques."

"No, please don't."

Danielle ignored her and gave the operator the number in Bruges. "If he wants to end such a beautiful love between you, he will have to tell you directly. You cannot be like a Molinard and refuse to talk."

"But Danielle, I don't want to talk to him."

"You must see this from my point of view, my very selfish point of view. For you it is simply a love affair, *fini.* I have experience with these things. One is miserable for days, sometimes weeks, but then there is always someone else. Men are like taxis. If you miss one, there is always another one to come by to take you where you want to go. You are very pretty, and so you will not suffer a very long time. But for me, I may be forced to endure Simone in my very house. This is a grave matter. You may wish to give Jacques to her without a fight, but I will not."

"Then I think you will have to find him another taxi," said Ariane. Despite her pain, she had to smile at the irrepressible girl.

"No! You are the only taxi that will take him to happiness."

"I wish you would think of something other than a taxi to compare me to," Ariane said.

"*Ma chère* taxi. No, it is good, such a comparison. You are ready to go off in all directions. *Allô?*" she said into the receiver. "*Oui, c'est moi, Danielle. Jacques est là? Non?*" She frowned and shot a worried glance at Ariane. "*Non, très bien, merci. Au revoir.*"

"Well?" asked Ariane, anxious to know what the servant had said.

Danielle sank down in a chair, throwing her arms up in despair. "He is *chez* Simone."

At Simone's! Already exhausted from a night without sleep and a day of sightseeing, Ariane could not bear the thought of dining out in one of the gay cafés on the Left Bank as Danielle had suggested earlier that day.

"Oh, *ma chère amie*," cooed Danielle. "Do not worry. I know that when one is disappointed in one's hopes, it is not possible to take joy from what seem to be frivolous pleasures. And it is especially hard in Paris, where everyone else always seems to be in love. I will order some food for us to eat here in the room, for I feel it is important for us to talk."

Ariane's spirits brightened somewhat fifteen minutes later when a white-jacketed hotel employee pushed a beautifully set table, complete with white linen tablecloth, into the room. On it were an assortment of croissants and brioches, a yellowish bread that was one of Ariane's favorite foods, and several types of jams. A large silver teapot and a bowl of carnations added to her sense of being deliciously spoiled.

"I don't know about you," said Danielle, "but when I feel so depressed that I think I don't ever want to face the world again, or at least not face it for several days"—a quick smiled brightened her gamine face—"I find it most comforting to bundle into my pajamas and dressing gown, as you say, and eat my favorite meal, breakfast. A late breakfast, that is!" Here she was able to get a laugh out of Ariane, who never would have thought of breakfast as anything even remotely known to a sleepyhead like Danielle.

"Now we must talk seriously," continued Danielle.

"There is something not right about this *affaire Molinard*. It is the girl in the green dress that bothers me."

"That bothered Simone, too," said Ariane.

"Yes, do you see?"

"What?" Ariane did not understand where Danielle's remarks were leading.

"If Simone loves Jacques, as she says, why would she go into so jealous a rage about a girl in a green dress?"

"Well, she was quite attractive—beautiful, in fact," pointed out Ariane.

"But the fact remains—Simone was *jealous*."

"That's understandable. Someone Jean-Paul had been engaged to—"

"No, not just jealous," interjected Danielle, eager for Ariane to understand. "A *rage* of jealousy. Don't you see?"

Ariane shook her head. Danielle spoke again. "It is a proven fact that one doesn't get jealous to such a degree unless one is strongly in love."

"Then you think Simone is still in love with Jean-Paul Molinard?" Ariane found it hard to believe anyone could love such a man, especially if one compared him to Jacques. Yet she considered Danielle's hypothesis. Was jealousy an indisputable product of love? Recently she had suffered her own excruciating pains of jealous rage with Jacques, but never had she been jealous of Bud. Even in the privacy of her own mind, Ariane hesitated to complete the thought. Hard as it was to admit that Bud might not have loved her, it was even more difficult to consider that she had not loved him.

"Yes, I *do* think so, *ma petite*, and I also think that you've spent too much time thinking about this whole thing today. Now I will treat you to something Americans always enjoy here in France—we will watch old American television shows, all dubbed conveniently into French, and we will laugh at how the French words fit perfectly the motions of the mouths speaking English, and then we will get some much-needed close-eye!"

Ariane laughed at Danielle's crazed version of the English "shut-eye," and definitely felt better. Danielle had given her hope—and that was something she'd thought she'd run out of.

The telephone ringing in the hotel suite the next morning jarred them awake. Ariane quickly picked up the receiver, knowing how much Danielle treasured her morning sleep. To her surprise and great pleasure, it was Tante Yvette.

"I'm sorry to call so early," she said cheerfully, "but I am at the airport, about to take a flight to Paris. Uncle Louis's mother is much better, but he is going to remain here until tomorrow. We can have lunch together today!"

So at noon Ariane and her favorite aunt began catching up on the years that had passed since they'd last seen each other. The hours flew by as they exchanged snapshots, recipes for Ariane's mother, and a swatch of the new rug her mother wanted Yvette to approve. The sisters had been very close as children and now wrote to each other constantly. Ariane thought painfully that theirs was the sort of relationship she could have had with Danielle.

Yvette, being sensitive to Ariane's feelings, carefully skirted the subject of Bud, but Ariane would have gladly talked about him if only to avoid her aunt's probing questions about the Valbonne family. "It was a beautiful old house with gardens and a stable. You would have loved the antique furniture, Tante Yvette."

Her aunt was not interested in the furniture. "But your mother said in her last letter that there was a young man who trained horses. You were there helping him?"

"Yes, for a while." Her cheeks reddened.

"And he was handsome, this man?" Nothing escaped Yvette's shrewd eyes.

"Quite good looking in a rugged sort of way."

"Ah. So perhaps there was something a little more interesting than the horses, eh?"

"Well, we were always busy with the horses. His sister Danielle and I became quite good friends."

"You were staying at the house of a handsome bachelor and you did not go out with him?"

"Just to do some sightseeing." Ariane hated lying to her aunt, but she certainly could not reveal the full nature of her relationship with Jacques. In days the news would be across the Atlantic and in her mother's hand.

Tante Yvette shook her head. "Ariane, you cannot continue to live in the past. I have wanted to be delicate, but your husband is no more with us. You must soon start to consider the rest of your life. You are still young and very beautiful—" The telephone interrupted her speech. "It's for you, Ariane—one of the Valbonne men. Father or son, he did not say."

Hope fluttered in her chest. Was Danielle home already? Had she spoken to Jacques?

But it was the elder Monsieur Valbonne. "I hope your aunt's mother-in-law has recovered her health."

"Yes, the crisis seems to have passed. My uncle is coming home tomorrow."

"I am happy to hear that. You will let me know if I can be of any assistance to you."

"That's very kind of you, Monsieur Valbonne."

"But the reason I called you was to thank you for encouraging my daughter to pursue the School of Economics."

"Oh, I was sure you'd be pleased!" Ariane was proud of Danielle for speaking to her father without Ariane's presence to boost her morale, especially after his remarks in the restaurant the night before.

"How very pleased, I cannot begin to tell you. When Danielle was a little girl, she showed acute interest in my work, but I never thought of her making a career. And lately I have been very worried that she seems to have no interest in marriage and was leading so aimless a life. It was good for her to see a woman who had a profession and who was not afraid of hard work. If it had not been for your friendship and support, I am afraid she would never have had the courage to tell me."

"You give me too much credit. Danielle is a wonderful person. I know she is going to do well."

"I hope so, with all my heart. And perhaps it is not my place to say, but Danielle seems convinced that you and Jacques will be getting married. I just wanted you to know that there is not another woman I would rather have for a daughter-in-law."

Ariane was moved. "Monsieur Valbonne, if only Danielle were right. Your saying that means a great deal to me. The Valbonnes will always be among my dearest friends."

She could hardly face the probing eyes of her aunt when she hung up the phone. "That was Danielle's father, and he called to thank me for encouraging her to go to an economics school."

"That's all? You have tears in your eyes about an economics school?"

Fortunately the doorbell was ringing and Ariane did not have to answer. But to her dismay it was none other than Jean-Paul Molinard, and he was wasting no time in describing his mission to Tante Yvette. "I would like very much to escort your beautiful niece to dinner."

"I really couldn't go," said Ariane quickly. "My aunt just arrived from Marseilles and . . ."

Yvette took in the cultured appearance of this handsome man in order to make a detailed report to her sister later. Ariane was sure that she did not fail to notice the manicured nails. Those alone would take up several sentences. "Ariane," Yvette said in an authoritative tone, "I want you to go out tonight and have a good time. Don't worry about leaving me here. Uncle Louis will arrive tomorrow morning and I must take care of the laundry and a million other details."

"But Tante Yvette—"

"Ariane, it's about time you stopped acting like a bereaved widow. Don't give me that pained expression. Your mother wrote me that Uncle Louis and I should encourage you to go out. So that is exactly what I am doing. This nice young man has very cordially invited you out to dine, and you would disappoint him if you did not go."

While Ariane searched for another excuse, Jean-Paul took her silence for acceptance. "Then it is settled," he said happily. "My car is waiting outside."

"But I'm not even dressed for dinner." It was a weak excuse, but the only one she could muster up.

"You are looking ravishing to me," said Jean-Paul, "but I will be happy to wait if you wish to change."

Ariane sighed. She had been trapped, but there was no sense in making herself any more appealing to Jean-Paul. He would only interpret it as meaning she wanted to look pretty for him. The last thing he needed was encouragement. She grabbed a coat and let Jean-Paul usher her to the door.

"A little lipstick would not be a crime," whispered Tante Yvette, but her niece seemed not to hear.

If Jean-Paul Molinard had seemed insufferable at lunch, he was even more so at dinner without the mediating influence of the Valbonnes. "I'm awfully tired, Jean-Paul," she managed finally after the last remains of the chocolate mousse he had recommended were removed from the table. "I've been working the Valbonne horses for the past few weeks and I guess I'm just physically exhausted."

"You work horses?"

"Yes. I train them."

"How interesting."

"Yes, it is."

"Simone despises horses."

"I know."

"I don't care for them either, but Pierre is fond of them. Did you see him ride? I don't believe there is a child who can ride better."

"You could be right. He's very talented."

"Pity that horses are so dirty. Do you really enjoy that sort of work?"

She was at her wits' end. Not only had he ignored her hint about going home, but he had pulled the wrong trigger. "Jean-Paul, do you realize that throughout an entire

meal, this is the very first time you've asked me about my
life?"

He seemed surprised, then defensive. "I asked you
where you bought the dress."

"The dress—always the superficial! The dress is not
me, what I am, what I do."

"I'm afraid I do not understand. If I have offended
you . . . Simone and I always talk about these things and
she is always interested."

Ariane shook her head. It was useless to attempt an
explanation. To Jean-Paul Molinard, Simone was perfection, so everything fit into one of two categories: what
Simone liked and what Simone didn't like. In his own silly
way he was every bit as in love with his wife as she was
with Jacques.

How she ached for Jacques at that moment. Never again
would anyone be able to read her thoughts. There had
been no lack of interesting subjects to discuss, and there
had always been their mutual passion for horses. The
world, she was beginning to fear, was full of narrow,
boring men like Jean-Paul Molinard. Only Jacques was
unique, the one all-encompassing love in her life. And she
had let him slip away. If she'd had any courage, she would
have stayed in Bruges and fought it out with Simone. But
it was too late.

"Back so early?" Tante Yvette was surprised to see
Ariane returning from dinner only a few hours after she'd
left the apartment. Normally she would have been more
concerned that her niece seemed not to have had a good
time, but a promising omen for Ariane's increasing social
life had come through in her absence. "Well," she said,
her eyes twinkling, "no matter how you treat them, there
always seems to be another ready to step up. A young
man called here for you just after you left."

Ariane's heart was pounding wildly.

"It was Jacques Valbonne."

"Oh, Tante Yvette!" She hugged her bewildered aunt.
"Did he say he'd call back? Am I supposed to call him

back?" Her questions tumbled out quickly, breathlessly.

"He was a little rude-sounding, Ariane. I didn't know . . . well, I hope I did not spoil anything." Quick to see that the phone call was of some romantic importance, Yvette realized that her first suspicions had been correct—it was the horseman.

Ariane froze. "What did you say to him? You didn't tell him I was out with Jean-Paul Molinard, did you?"

"Not exactly—well, not at first. I said that you had gone to dinner with a young man you had met with his sister and father. He asked it if it was Jean-Paul Molinard. Thinking it was a friend of his, I said yes."

Ariane clutched the back of a chair to steady herself; her mouth was dry. "What did he say then?"

"That is when he became rude."

"Rude?"

"Well, more angry than rude. I tried to be polite and ask him if he wanted to leave a message for you. At first he said no, then he changed his mind."

"Oh dear, Tante Yvette, what did he say?"

"Here, I wrote it down." She handed a scrap of paper to Ariane. "I always believe in writing things down so I don't forget. Your mother got me into that habit."

Ariane's hand shook as she read the note: "Tell Ariane that she has made an eloquent statement with her actions. She need not return the call."

"Oh, Tante Yvette, please, how does one dial direct to Bruges?"

Danielle was at the other end of the line within seconds. "Oh, Ariane, *tu ne sais pas ce qui est arrivé!*"

"Danielle, slowly or in English, please. I cannot understand a word when you speak so fast."

"It is all *fou*—crazy. The night that Jacques stayed away—he was at the hospital. It was Pierre. He found some poison for the rats and ate it!"

"Is he all right?"

"Yes, but so miserably unhappy a little boy—so very confused, *le pauvre*. But that is why Jacques was at Simone's when we called from Paris. She calls to Jean-Paul every hour but he does not answer, nor does he return her calls."

"I can't imagine why he wouldn't return the calls if he knew Pierre were so sick."

"He doesn't know, Ariane. And Simone will not leave a complete message. She insists that she must tell him herself. Don't ask me why. They are both so silly. You saw that. But I finally spoke to Jacques, and he felt so bad that you had left thinking he had made love to Simone. That he is why he called you right away. But then your aunt said—it was not true, was it? Ariane, you could not have gone out with that ridiculous Molinard?"

"I did."

"I do not believe it!"

Ariane explained the circumstances. And in relating the incidents, she realized bleakly that she could have been firmer in her refusal to go out with him.

"Jacques was an *orage*—how you say?"

"A storm."

"A hurricane storm. He left the house right after he spoke to your aunt, and I do not know where he has gone. But it is not to Simone."

"How do you know?"

"I already called there."

"What shall I do?" Ariane asked her friend in desperation.

Danielle responded without hesitation "Call Papa and see if you can get his pilot to fly you here."

"I couldn't do that! Besides, to show up there—Jacques would think . . ."

"No, you *must* come. There is another problem, too. Even if you do not want to see Jacques. It's Wicked Willie."

"Willie? Is he okay? His spavin is back?"

"It is not the spavin. His legs are fine, but he does not eat, and he is not sick that I can see. He just will not eat. So you see, you must come here quickly."

"I'll catch the next train out of Paris and be there tonight."

"I'll be at the station to pick you up. I know the train—it will arrive after midnight, but you must hurry to catch it."

Ariane tried to explain the recent events to Tante Yvette as she threw her clothes back into the suitcase, but her excuses were not holding up to Yvette's inquisitorial barrage. "For a horse you can wait until morning, Ariane. I cannot let you get onto a train at this hour of the night."

"But he won't eat."

"Your mother and I were raised on a farm. A horse can live for many days without food. Now tell me, is it this Jacques Valbonne?"

"Well, yes."

"And *he* cannot wait until the morning?"

"You don't understand; there has been a terrible misunderstanding."

"A misunderstanding will not get any worse if it waits a few hours until daylight."

Ariane latched her suitcase and sped toward the door. "Which train station do I go to, Tante Yvette?"

Her aunt sighed. "To be young and in love. I had almost forgotten. One does not listen to reason." She grabbed her car keys. "I will drive you to the station."

Chapter Thirteen

ARIANE WAS BEGINNING to regret that she had not swallowed her pride and asked Monsieur Valbonne for the use of his private jet, or that she had not at least caught a night flight to Brussels. It was well after midnight when her train pulled into the Bruges station. She tried her best to freshen up with lipstick and eye liner, but her hair still hung limply, and she knew that her exhaustion showed on her face.

Fortunately Danielle had called the station to make sure the train would arrive on time and was there to meet her. "Jacques has still not returned. I called all the bars in Zeebrugge and Zutte, though I don't know why—he rarely goes to bars. But the yacht club in Zeebrugge said he was there for one drink of cognac, then left."

"How is Willie?" Ariane was not sure whether she was more concerned about her horse or the whereabouts of Jacques.

"Willie ate a little more grain tonight," said Danielle brightly, "but only if I fed him from my hand. He still will not look at his hay."

"He did this once before when I went up to the Adirondacks with a friend for a week. Bud had a terrible time with him. He scarcely ate a thing until I returned, then he acted as though nothing had happened."

"Then you think it is a problem *psychologique*?" asked Danielle with obvious relief.

"Let's hope so." She was anxious to get to him and see, but as they were driving through town she suddenly made Danielle stop the car.

"Jacques is at Gruuthuse, I'm sure of it. Do you know the way from here?"

"It's only a few blocks, but what an odd place to look for someone. What would he be doing there this time of night?"

"Let's go by there and see, please—it won't take but a minute to check."

The area near Gruuthuse was not very well illuminated, and they had to park along the canal some distance away. When they finally arrived at the narrow bridge it was dark and deserted. "This place makes me to shiver," said Danielle. "Did you know about the skeletons they found in there?"

Ariane was too distraught to give much thought to ghosts and legends. She only wanted to find Jacques. But Danielle appealed to her sense of reason. "He must come home eventually. If not tonight, then he will be home in the morning to work the horses. It could be the end of the world and Jacques would still get up in the morning and work his horses."

What Ariane also knew was that he would not go to sleep at night without checking them. With any luck she might be able to intercept him at the stable.

His car was not at the house when they drove up. But Ariane felt happier just being back at the ancient Valbonne estate again. There was no doubt it felt like home.

Danielle bid her a good night while Ariane ran quickly down to the stables.

Several of the horses stuck their heads out of their stalls to greet her; Willie shook his mane and nickered loudest of all. She grabbed a handful of grain and went into his stall. "Yes, I'm back here again, you crazy, silly Willie. I couldn't leave you for very long."

Willie nibbled the grain, careful to pick it up without biting her hand. The hay was overflowing his feeder. It was obvious he had not touched it for days. She took a handful and gave it to him. At first he turned away, then as she spoke to him he took a small tentative bite, then another. While continuing to eat he nuzzled happily against her, putting his head down so that she could scratch behind his ears. "Didn't that nasty man scratch behind your ears?" she asked him softly. "At least your bog spavin's all gone."

Willie brushed by her and put himself in a position so that she could scratch his shoulders. He hung his head down, his upper lip hanging loose and his eyes closed in ecstasy. "Poor, poor Willie. You mean he didn't scratch your back either? Of all the indignities you've had to suffer!"

"He's not the only one here who's had indignities to suffer." She heard Jacques's voice behind her.

Ariane wheeled around to see him outside the stall watching her.

"How long have you been standing there?" She was so flushed and nervous, it was all she could manage to say.

"So you don't think I've been taking proper care of Willie, eh?"

"Oh, I didn't mean . . . it's just . . . ." Willie, noting that she had stopped scratching his back, nudged her gently.

"He's trying to tell you something."

She automatically began scratching again. "There's been a terrible misunderstanding, Jacques."

"Do you want to talk about it, or are you going to stand there all night and scratch that animal's back?"

"Sorry, Will." She gave the horse a kiss on the end of his warm nose. "We'll continue this later."

Stepping out of the stall, she got a better look at Jacques. His black hair was disheveled, as though he'd been out in the wind, and he was wearing jeans and a thick leather jacket lined with lamb's wool.

"I had Danielle take me to Gruuthuse, thinking you might be there."

"I was. I saw you there."

"But why didn't you . . . ?"

He didn't answer. She followed him around the stable until they reached the red room, where they had first made love.

"When you called at my aunt's, I had just gone to dinner for a few hours. I didn't want to go, but my aunt practically threw me at Jean-Paul. Believe me, nothing happened."

"Were you disappointed?" he said sarcastically. He pinned her with his penetrating green eyes for a moment, then unlocked the door. The curtain of bottle caps clinked behind them.

"I never wanted to start anything with Jean-Paul Molinard. He is an insufferable, boring person."

Jacques did not answer her but set himself to the task of building a fire in the old stone fireplace. "Before I went Gruuthuse I drove up to the North Sea at Zeebrugge and walked in the sand. It's cold out there on the beach at night," he said distantly, his back to her.

Was he going to hear her out? Had she made this long trip in the middle of the night for nothing? She trembled at his coldness, which seemed to increase even as the fire began to heat the small room. "Jacques, I came back here to apologize for running off that morning. How was I to know that you were at the hospital? I could only imagine that you were spending the night with Simone and that you'd lied to me."

Jacques wheeled quickly around to face her. "You had absolutely no trust in me at all! Not even enough trust to wait to hear what I had to say." His green eyes reflected the fury of the crackling flames.

"Trust?" She said incredulously. "Don't be a hypocrite. How willing were you to trust me when you heard that I had gone to dinner with Jean-Paul Molinard?"

"You only went out with Jean-Paul to show me you could attract Simone's husband—to show Simone. Are you glad that you hurt her?"

"But how did she know—unless you told her." Ariane herself could almost not believe how strong her anger was.

"She called Jean-Paul in Paris, and the maid said that he was out with you. The only reason for him to leave a specific name would be to inflict some pain on Simone. As if she did not have enough to suffer!"

"The petty little man! Yes, of course he wanted to hurt her. Both the Molinards are like that. They must stay awake nights thinking of ways to do each other in. But don't accuse me of such nonsense, Jacques. Did you know that Simone was throwing *your* name at Jean-Paul—telling him that the two of you were going to be married and that you were going to adopt Pierre?"

"That's not true. Simone would not lie like that!"

"But *I* would?" Ariane was standing now, shaking with a fury she did not know she possessed. "You talk about trust and in the same breath you accuse me of lying. I can see now where I stand. You are just like Jean-Paul Molinard. You see nothing but womanly perfection in Simone, as though she were not capable of base manipulation. Well, she has gotten her way with all of you, tangled you all up in her little web so tightly that you cannot see the way out. But if that is what you want, fine! Go to your perfect Simone who would not lie. Go marry her and adopt the son you think is yours anyway."

She walked through the bottle-cap curtain and out into the night. Jacques followed right behind her. "I do not have any intention of marrying Simone or adopting Pierre. You cannot believe what Pierre said that day."

"I heard the same story from Jean-Paul. So did your sister. Will you also accuse her of lying?"

She pulled her hand away from his and began to run. Suddenly she wanted to be far away from Jacques, from the Valbonne house. But he caught up with her before she passed the stables. "Ariane, we are not finished talking."

"I'm tired of talking. You do not listen. There is no sense in talking to a wall."

"You are right. Talking will never solve anything between us. I have a better solution." She was startled to detect a smile in his voice and wheeled around to face him. "Come on, we'll go for a ride."

"You're not going to saddle up horses at this hour of the night." She was sure he was kidding, but he had turned his back on her and was walking resolutely to the stable.

"Night is a good time to ride, Ariane," he called over his shoulder. "And there is no need to saddle. We'll go bareback."

Within seconds he had bridled a large thoroughbred gelding and was leading the sleepy horse out of the stable.

Ariane started to laugh in spite of herself. "You are completely crazy."

"No crazier than you for jumping on a train tonight." He lifted her onto the horse's broad back, then vaulted on behind her.

No matter how furious she was at Jacques, it was a thrilling sensation to lean tightly against his warm, hard chest as the powerful animal moved under them. His strong arms encircled her as he held the reins. Without a saddle she could feel the horse's every muscle straining against her inner thighs. She locked her knees in close to the withers and held lightly on to the horse's long black mane.

Jacques kept an eye on the black trail below them, looking over her shoulder. The familiar sight of his sculptured features, his shining green eyes under the dark lashes, gave her a feeling of well-being. She knew in that moment that she would always love this man. No matter what happened, he was all that was important in this world. Not even her adored Wicked Willie was as precious to her.

When they reached the straight section of the trail, he urged the horse forward into a canter. The animal was graceful for his large size and lifted off the ground with ease, enjoying this midnight ride as much as his passengers. Jacques brushed her smooth cheek with his lips as they flew across the ground. She glanced up at him and smiled. He was wearing the expression that she knew appeared only in moments of ecstasy or when he was on a horse. At that moment the two were combined.

By the time they had returned to their red room in back of the stable, the fire had warmed it in readiness for them. The ride had been foreplay; the sensuous, even rhythms of the horse had teased and caressed, moved their hips back and forth into a maddening imitation of the love act. Their lips now met hungrily, with a dizzying passion that would ordinarily have come later.

Clothes were flung helter-skelter around the room in their desperate need to feel the texture of skin, to taste it. She longed to wrap her legs around him as she had the horse, to feel the completion of his love, but Jacques did not want to hurry, even now as their bodies cried out to make them one.

His roving hands were like magnets, drawing shock waves every place he touched and caressed. Even the bottoms of her feet sent sparks to the center of her being.

"Riding for us, Ariane," he whispered, "is like making love. It *is* love—what our lives will be like together."

"Oh, how I love you, Jacques," she moaned as he rolled her on top of him. They were insatiable, mad with an abandoned joy they knew was theirs forever. She did not know whether she was laughing or crying, only that she never wanted it to end.

By the time they left their little room, the icy morning winds were rearranging the heavy Flemish clouds above them in a rose-lavender sky. Ariane felt as though she were floating on one of them, for her legs did not seem long enough or steady enough to touch the ground.

"Look, Jacques!" she cried as she reached Willie's stall. "He's eaten everything in his feeder!" She brought him some more feed, which he began to devour hungrily.

Jacques slipped an arm around her and kissed the top of her toussled auburn hair. "He could not eat because he missed you. I was sure ot it. I hardly ate anything either the whole time you were gone."

After attending to the horses, they climbed the stairs wearily and collapsed across her bed without bothering to remove their clothes again. Within minutes they were both sleeping soundly, arms and legs entwined, for they were still not ready to relinquish the glorious feeling of closeness.

Ariane dreamed a strange dream—of a moonlight ride across a meadow, Jacques behind her on the horse. There were angry voices somewhere in the distance that were intruding on her dream. She opened her eyes and sighed. Finding herself stretched across her bed at the Valbonne house, her clothes from the night before still on, she suddenly remembered and smiled. It had not been a dream after all. But the voices coming from the terrace downstairs . . . One of them was Jacques's. She saw his leather jacket thrown carelessly over the green armchair. As she went to the window she touched it, and a rush of sensations filled her. Anything that belonged to Jacques was magical, she acknowledged happily. But why was he speaking so harshly? And who was the woman with him?

The white Mercedes was parked in the driveway. Sitting on the balustrade was a tiny speck of an unhappy-looking little boy watching his mother and Jacques argue.

The French was too rapid and the voices too far away for Ariane to understand, so after running a brush through her hair she went downstairs without bothering to change clothes. She would have burst in upon them on the terrace, but as she reached the dining room doors she heard Simone say, "So much for the faithfulness of your red-haired *Américaine*! Jean-Paul told me that after he took her to dinner she stayed with him all night."

Ariane slid back behind the curtains so that she would not be seen and listened.

"Jean-Paul is lying to you, Simone."

"You do not want to believe anything bad about that girl, even when I warned you she was treacherous. First she tried to come between you and me, and when that failed she tried to cause a rift between you and Pierre. Now she is not satisfied with that either and she wants my Jean-Paul."

"How could she come between you and me when we are only good friends, Simone? You talk as though we had become lovers again."

"Jacques," Simone said with horror. "Pierre is right there."

"That poor child has heard too much for his age as it is. You have already filled his small head with silly lies. Why did you tell him that you and I were going to be married?"

"I never told him that."

"And you told Jean-Paul."

"That is ridiculous! What an accusation!"

Pierre slipped off the balustrade and ran down to the stable. "Pierre!" Simone called after him.

"Let him go. He is better off with the simple good-natured animals," said Jacques bitterly. "You have proved yourself quite a competent mother."

Simone was barely holding back her tears. "I . . . I had to tell him *something*, Jacques," she finally said. "There had to be a reason he was not seeing the father he loved so much."

"Tell me the truth, Simone." His voice had a hard edge, and he had taken her by the shoulders and was holding her tightly. Ariane felt the power of his grip even though she was only watching them. "Is Jean-Paul Pierre's father or am I?"

"I don't know—honestly, Jacques, I don't know."

"You do."

Ariane could see the menacing scowl on Jacques's face. She had experienced his wrath and knew how intimidating it could be.

He shook her ever so slightly. "The *truth*, Simone!" he demanded.

"All right!" She released herself from his powerful grip. "Pierre is *Jean-Paul's* son!" she said with a sob.

"And all these years you've let me wonder," he said with disgust, "let me feel the guilt."

She wheeled on him, her blond hair flying loose from its usual restraints. Ariane thought she looked like a madwoman. Never had she seen Simone so out of control. "That's exactly what I wanted you to feel. How do you think I felt when all my life I had thought we would be married. The horses, you said. But I knew it was just an excuse. You did not love me. That was the real reason you did not marry me. The day you told me I thought to myself, 'I am going to find a man who looks like Jacques Valbonne and have his child whether I am married or not. And all his life Jacques will wonder.' I wanted your insides to twist with pain every time you looked at my child. I wanted you to know what might have been yours."

Jacques seemed to be seeing this woman clearly for the first time in his life, unmasked of all her perfect beauty. "No wonder Pierre tried to kill himself, a child that was conceived as an instrument of revenge. God, how you amused yourself playing on my guilt, Simone."

"I was never amused," she said sadly. "The fates played tricks with me, Jacques. In looking for a man who resembled you, I found a man who taught me what it really was to love. We are very much alike, Jean-Paul and I, and we were very happy, until that Hélène Pélisier came between us in Cannes. He was ready to throw away all we had built together for that horrible woman! And now he is in the arms of that American girl. I am sorry for you, Jacques, for she has deceived you just as Jean-Paul has deceived me."

"No, Simone," he said softly. "Ariane and I are going to be married."

"You will marry her after she has been with my husband?"

"She was not with Jean-Paul last night."

"But he told me this morning that she was there."

Ariane decided that it was time she made her presence known. "Jean-Paul lied to you," she said calmly as she walked out onto the terrace. "I was here with Jacques all night."

Simone's mouth fell open as though she had seen a ghost. "But you were in Paris. I know you left with Danielle—"

"I went to dinner with Jean-Paul last night, then I took a train to Bruges. Listen to me, Simone. Jean-Paul still loves you very much. He did nothing but talk about you.

Don't you see that he is trying to make you jealous by saying he was with me? He is so sure that you are here with Jacques he feels he has to get even. He never spent the night with Hélène; he hasn't spent the night with anyone. He is too much in love with you to even talk to another woman about anything but you, and Pierre."

Simone stared at Ariane in a state of shock. The glaring reality of Jean-Paul's lie was as startling as Ariane's revelation that he still loved her. "Are you sure that he still loves me?"

"Why don't you call and ask him?"

She shook her head vehemently. "No. Not after what he said to me this morning."

"Don't you see how much he must love you to make up this story about me being with him?"

Simone considered what Ariane said for only a few moments. It was too good a theory to reject. She turned toward the stables. "Pierre!" she yelled, and a small face appeared from the window of one of the stalls. "Pierre, come get ready. We are going home."

He came toward them at a shuffling gate. "I want to stay here with the horses, *Maman*."

"But we are going *home*, darling. Home to Paris. Home to Papa."

Pierre looked up at his mother with surprise. "Really? Home to Papa? Are you sure he does not hate us?"

"Yes, my love, I'm sure. He wants us to come home."

Pierre could not conceal his joy. Already there was some color in his cheeks as he ran to the Mercedes.

Ariane and Jacques watched the car drive swiftly down the lane, then looked at each other in amazement. "All those years," he mumbled, but Ariane's lips were on his before he could continue.

"So much noise so early in the morning," said Danielle, yawning at the door. She was still in a long yellow bathrobe, her blond curls in disarray.

"It's almost noon, Dany," her brother teased. "What are you going to do when you are in business and must get up for the stock market opening?"

"I shall make them pass a law that makes it illegal for the stock market to open before noon. Now, let us have some *tartines* and discuss this wedding. It must be appropriate. My suggestion is that you get married on horseback."

"That is appropriate," Jacques said with a smile.

"I will be the maid of honor and Wicked Willie will be the best man. I shall invite Dmitry to play the wedding march on his balalaika, and we will have the entire ceremony at the Lake of Love on the bridge so that you can kiss while the swans pass beneath. Because, you know, you two will love each other forever."

Jacques and Ariane looked at each other and began to laugh as they recalled their first kiss and the enchantment that had enveloped them. Whether or not they could attribute it to the magical swans or to the magic of horses they were certain of one thing: theirs was a love that would last forever.

Introducing a unique new concept in romance novels!
Every woman deserves a…

Second Chance at Love ™

You'll revel in the settings, you'll delight
in the heroines, you may even fall in love with the
magnetic men you meet in the pages of…

SECOND CHANCE AT LOVE

Look for three new
novels of lovers lost and found coming every
month from Jove! Available now:

____05703-7	FLAMENCO NIGHTS (#1) by Susanna Collins	$1.75
____05637-5	WINTER LOVE SONG (#2) by Meredith Kingston	$1.75
____05624-3	THE CHADBOURNE LUCK (#3) by Lucia Curzon	$1.75
____05777-0	OUT OF A DREAM (#4) by Jennifer Rose	$1.75
____05878-5	GLITTER GIRL (#5) by Jocelyn Day	$1.75
____05863-7	AN ARTFUL LADY (#6) by Sabina Clark	$1.75
____05694-4	EMERALD BAY (#7) by Winter Ames	$1.75
____05776-2	RAPTURE REGAINED (#8) by Serena Alexander	$1.75
____05801-7	THE CAUTIOUS HEART (#9) by Philippa Heywood	$1.75